Shatila
Stories

First published in 2018 by
Peirene Press Ltd
17 Cheverton Road
London N19 3BB
United Kingdom
www.peirenepress.com

ISBN 978-1-908670-48-9

Designed by Sacha Davison Lunt
Photos (cover & flaps): Paul Romans
Photos (inside): All by Paul Romans, except p9 by Omar Khaled Ahmad
Typeset by Tetragon, London
Printed and bound by T J International, Cornwall

Peirene

Shatila
Stories

OMAR KHALED AHMAD
NIBAL ALALO
SAFA KHALED ALGHARBAWI
OMAR ABDELLATIF ALNDAF
RAYAN MOHAMAD SUKKAR
SAFIYA BADRAN
FATIMA OMAR GHAZAWI
SAMIH MAHMOUD
HIBA MAREB

TRANSLATED FROM THE ARABIC
BY NASHWA GOWANLOCK

'Don't talk
about the
camp unless
you know it.'

Introduction

At the beginning of 2017 I approached the Lebanese-based charity Basmeh & Zeitooneh (which translates as 'The Smile & the Olive'). This NGO runs community centres in a number of refugee camps, including Shatila in Beirut. I wanted to find a group of Syrian writers, teach them the principles of storytelling and then publish a book of their work. I had set my mind on Shatila – the place made infamous by the 1982 massacre. This camp was founded in 1949 for 3,000 Palestinians but now houses up to 40,000 refugees following the Syrian crisis. I was clear in my mind that I didn't want flight stories from the writers. These have been covered enough by our media. I wanted to address something else, something that comes from my experience as a writer of stories: the power of collaborative imagination to open up new ways of remembering and from that, perhaps, a vision for the future.

When I start a new novel I have a vague idea of what I want to explore. In the course of writing, this idea becomes clearer. Images emerge, characters materialize, a plot evolves. Yet something is not right. So I rewrite, revise, add and cut, until the story is finished and has turned into a compelling read. Only when the book is complete do I truly understand what the story is about. The real creative motivation is always different from the (conscious) idea I had at the beginning. Writing the book has made me see something different, made me understand something I didn't know before.

I don't work alone. My partner is always my first reader. He reads each draft with an eye on the mechanics of the story. He doesn't care about the idea I'm trying to express. He cares if the story makes sense within its own logic. If it jars, I need to find a solution. It is this collaboration between my partner and myself, between the editor and the writer, that allows the story to find its own momentum, to express what it wants to express, and not whatever idea I had in my mind at the start. In this way, I as the writer can go beyond myself to become the vessel for something far larger, something unforeseen.

Armed with that knowledge, I arrived in Shatila last July. I had brought with me the London-based Syrian editor Suhir Helal. Over the previous six months, Suhir had helped me to brush up my Arabic and together we had worked out a programme for a three-day creative-writing workshop. In the meantime, Basmeh & Zeitooneh had run a pre-selection workshop and sent us twenty short writing samples. Each participant had been asked to say something about their name. Most of them struggled to write proper Arabic and organize their thoughts. Suhir and I didn't choose the best extracts. That was not an option. We chose the nine least bad. There was only one piece of writing that was interesting to read. In all honesty, both Suhir and I were worried before we even boarded the plane to Beirut.

When we arrived in Shatila our anxiety levels rose further. On the first day every single participant turned up late. Some had good reasons, because the life of a refugee can be chaotic, but for others timekeeping simply did not rank high among their priorities.

Shatila is governed by various opposing Palestinian groups. The Lebanese police do not enter the camp. If there is trouble, ambulances wait outside to receive the injured and the dead. Taxi drivers drop you a few streets away. And once inside I spotted many young men with handguns tucked into the back of their trousers. Yet normal life goes on here like anywhere else.

Over the course of the workshop the writers dealt with many challenges: mainly illnesses due to the atrocious hygiene in the overcrowded camp, but also the sudden deaths of family members. One participant's niece was killed by the low-hanging electrical cables, a grandmother slipped badly in one of the camp's muddy alleys and someone else's father died in Syria. These are just some of the reasons why participants skipped hours here and there during our precious three days. In addition, the room that we used at the Basmeh & Zeitooneh centre was as hot as a sauna, had no fans and shared a dividing wall with the primary school's dance class. And of course we had no computers, only pen and paper. The participants' ages ranged from eighteen to forty-two. Most had arrived in the camp from Syria during the last five years. Some had never completed their formal schooling and quite a few had never read a novel in their lives.

Halfway through the first day I hit rock bottom. This was never going to work, I thought. And I scolded myself for being so naive as to come here in the first place. I worried that we would produce a 'poor-refugee-can-also-write' kind of book. And a book like that would not make me proud. However, since I couldn't just walk out there and then, I decided to finish the three-day workshop first before pulling the plug on the project. But towards the end of the first day, something changed – inside myself and inside the writers. Their concentration and determination became palpable.

At the beginning, the writers were told that if they wrote a story which we were able to use in the book, they would receive an advance and royalties from the book sales. We also explained that the book would not be a collection of short stories but that we would take their stories and interweave them into a single narrative. That process would take place once their stories had been translated into English.

But first the writers had to produce good stories. The stories had to be set in Shatila and they had to be fiction. We concentrated on the most important aspects of story-writing. A story needs to have a begin-ning, a middle and an end. There must be an external conflict that changes the course of the story and an internal conflict within the main character. All characters have to want something, but only one thing. And, most importantly, a story is made up of concrete scenes, not abstract thoughts. Each day we read one short story by a well-known writer and completed a number of ten-minute writing exercises which we then read aloud and discussed.

There were many fiction-writing techniques that we did not teach, such as voice or points of view or even choice of tense. All of this I could manage in the editing process. In fact, I stressed that if the writers wanted they could change between past and present and switch between I and he and she. And if it was easier to write in colloquial Arabic they could do so. Or change between standardized written Arabic and vernacular, even within a paragraph. The most important task was to progress the story and bring Shatila alive on the page.

After the workshop each writer had six weeks to deliver a 4,000-word typed draft. During that time we kept in touch as a group via WhatsApp. There was only one person who delivered late, but even he delivered eventually. That's pretty impressive for any group, but especially for the Shatila writers. Most of them don't own a computer and so had to line up to use the one at the Basmeh & Zeitooneh centre. In addition, constant power cuts made any typing painfully slow.

We received four good stories and five interesting drafts. How was it possible for the course participants to apply what we were teaching them with so little practice and in such a short space of time? Why did they succeed where so many other creative-writing students fail?

'From my experience [with the workshop] I learned to live with my characters, to see them through my own eyes. I feel that through my characters I'm present in the story. The entire story is worked through my perspective,' said Safiya Badran.

'I've needed this opportunity for such a long time. I had a lot of thoughts to write down but I didn't know how to direct and express them. I have now learned how to organize my thoughts and I'm so happy to write the story,' said Omar Khaled Ahmad.

Omar and Safiya are two of the writers who delivered excellent stories. They brought to the project qualities that cannot be taught: enough humility to learn the craft and a terrific story to tell.

In October 2017, Suhir and I went back to Shatila and sat down with each of the nine writers individually to bring out the strengths in their stories. By that time we had an idea about the main conflict, which characters we could amalgamate and how to develop the subplots. With some writers we concentrated on sections or even just paragraphs from their stories; with others we helped them to bring out the voices of their characters or tighten the plot.

Afterwards, Nashwa Gowanlock translated everything into English. Working alongside her, Suhir and I combined the material into a coherent narrative.

When I embarked on this project, I had the idea that by pooling our imaginations we might be able to access something that would transcend the boundaries that surround individuals, nations and entire cultures. In the face of human catastrophes such as the Syrian refugee crisis, I wanted to see if it was possible to alter our thinking and so effect change.

Literature will never provide easy answers. And neither will *Shatila Stories*. But what it might do is give us an example of how we can connect with each other through one part of our shared human experience: our creativity.

MEIKE ZIERVOGEL

Publisher of Peirene Press
and editor of the Peirene Now! series

Shatila Alleys

We force ourselves to live here – forced not free.
The concrete buildings huddle in mismatched rows
And between them an alley snakes its way through.
We're stuck inside this maze. Above our heads
The electric cables tangle with themselves.
Beneath our feet the rain turns streets to mud.
The boy sits by the door too bored to play
His mother cries for a life she can't describe.
We have no home – no home but Shatila.
Spare us your good intentions, your quiet pity.
Instead, look up and raise your fist at the sky.

The Arrival

Chaos everywhere. Thundering sounds rip through my ears. I blink and blink again. I take snapshots with my eyes. Racing feet, dragging feet; old people, young people; cars of different colours, of different shapes; grey sky, swaying trees. Hundreds, thousands are waiting at the closed gate, paperwork in hand, hoping to pass through. They want to cross the border. A scene worthy of the Day of Reckoning. Worry and fear are paramount. A pallor has settled across everyone's face, no matter how dark or fair their complexion. Desperate eyes.

I bid farewell to the country that I have lived in since my very first day. We are leaving for a safer place. We are on our way from Damascus to Beirut.

The confusion around me helps to dispel anxious thoughts about the future. I distract myself by contemplating my reflection in the car window. The mirror image shows a young woman with large, tired eyes. She wears a brown scarf and a brown coat. My gaze travels down to her feet. The red winter boots look out of place considering the circumstances.

And so our journey begins. First to the Hermel border region, an agricultural area surrounded by mountains, with the River Asi running through it.

Afterwards all I will remember is the small white car we leave in and how we have to squeeze into the back seat, sitting on our hands because there is no room for our arms. I'm next to my younger brother, Adam. Next to Adam sit our parents. Marwan, my husband, is in the passenger seat beside the driver, who tries to deal with his fear by cracking jokes that no one pays any attention to. He has a black beard, wears glasses and uses a white rag to wipe the windscreen, which is fogging up from our breath. Eventually I can free my hands and I drape Marwan's black jacket around me, hoping it will form a barrier between my ears and the pounding of my heart.

Scenes of shooting and shouting and panic and fear and blood flicker through my mind, like watching an old television set connected to a faulty aerial. Yet I manage to fall asleep, and as I drift off I suddenly feel pleased that I'm able to do just that – close my eyes and succumb to oblivion. But soon I'm stirred again by the sound of a frightened dog. Every now and then, I hear the melodic call of a cricket trying to attract a mate. Then once more the night wraps me up in a black blanket.

'Thanks be to Allah for your safety.'

The driver's voice reaches me from far away, followed by my mother's gentle nudge: 'Reham, we're here.'

I get out of the car and walk towards the black door. Carefully, I slide my feet across the muddy ground. An old peasant woman greets us, laughter lines etched on her wrinkled face as she welcomes us into her home. We climb marble steps lit by the yellow glow of a lantern that brightens and dims as we move.

After only a few hours' sleep we are on the road again, long before sunrise. Our destination is the Shatila camp in Beirut, our new home.

We hope that Shatila will be our refuge. Because we believe blood is thicker than water. We know we will be living among fellow Palestinian refugees. And we are convinced that we won't feel like strangers.

I know very little about Shatila, only that it's a camp that was established in 1949 in the south of Beirut on agricultural land to house Palestinian refugees. In 1982 the area entered history as the site of the horrific massacre at Sabra and Shatila camps.

My husband, Marwan, has worked on a number of restoration projects in the Lebanese capital so he knows people who live in Shatila. We will stay with one of them for the first few days. But Marwan has promised that he will soon get us our own apartments, one for him and me and one for my parents and Adam.

Our attempts to convince a taxi driver to take us inside Shatila fail again and again. Eventually we are dropped in Jalool Land, the camp entrance. It's now seven in the morning and the streets of the camp are still asleep.

We approach a café where Marwan tells us we will meet his contact.

A young man, almost a boy still, about Adam's age, is scrubbing red paint off his fingers under a tap. As he's drying his hands he introduces himself as Muneef. He offers us coffee, which we gratefully accept. As we sip it, I notice from the corner of my eye how he takes a gun from a small shelf underneath the sink and slides it into the back of his trousers. For a second my heart stops. In a panic I glance at the others. Didn't we come here in order to escape from guns and violence and war? But no one except me seems to have noticed and Muneef appears friendly.

As we leave the café he tells us we'd be better off carrying our bags on our backs. At first I don't understand what he means, but with his next instruction it begins to make sense.

'Stomp your feet as you walk. It'll frighten the rats.'

Marwan has never mentioned rats!

Muneef has plenty of advice, behaving just like a good guide for tourists. He also informs us that today the electricity will be off from six to nine.

'That's good,' he says, nodding enthusiastically. 'Often it's out for much longer.'

We march through dim, muddy alleyways where hardly any light penetrates even though the sky above us is now brightening. Tangled electrical cables run everywhere above our heads and wrap themselves around water pipes, climbing up the precariously assembled buildings that look like giant matchboxes stacked on top of each other. I gasp at the sight of an exposed copper wire at the end of a sagging cable. Is it live? What if one of our heads skims it as we walk past? Suddenly I struggle to breathe. As if there's no oxygen left in these alleyways.

Three big fat rats cut across the path right in front of my feet, scurrying from one side alley to another, where they leap onto a towering rubbish heap. A thick, dark cloud of flies hovers above it. I shriek. Marwan throws me an angry glance, before looking at my parents with concern. Thankfully they are staring down, trying hard not to slip in this mud. We walk on. I see posters of former camp residents who were killed in the 1982 massacre. And there are many walls covered in graffiti. My eyes fall on a map of Palestine and slogans speaking of a heartfelt desire to return to the homeland. And then there are the flags, all relating to various political factions, including the green Hamas flags, the yellow Fatah ones and the black flags of the Palestinian Islamic Jihad. It dawns on me that the camp must be divided by allegiance to different factions.

Our group comes to a halt. Muneef has stopped in front of a huge, freshly painted slogan: *Don't talk about the camp unless you know it.*

'I painted it this morning.' He grins proudly. 'I'm fed up with people judging us when they don't even know the camp.'

We all nod. But I don't know what he's talking about. And I'm sure neither do my parents or Adam. Yet we don't dare to ask. Instead I see Adam throw a fearful glance at Muneef's gun in the back of his trousers.

Questions begin circling in my mind as we penetrate ever deeper into this maze of muddy alleys and low-hanging electrical cables. For a moment I turn my face upwards and catch a glimpse of the sky. I observe a flock of pigeons escaping.

Suddenly I am overwhelmed by a feeling that we are now like seeds buried deep in the dark earth. We have arrived in a prison which we have entered of our own free will, or so it appears. Sentenced without any charge.

Reham's Story

Back in Syria, the society I lived in was conservative. Men and women weren't allowed to mix, which made it difficult to meet the man of my dreams. Everyone was married off in a traditional manner: the mother of the groom would choose the bride for her son, as if the girl was just an object. And that is exactly what happened with me. Marwan's mother came to our house to inspect 'the goods' and then the traditional rituals were started for our engagement.

Marwan was a mechanical engineer. His financial situation was 'acceptable' and he was well educated and polite.

We hit it off straight away and that first month went by in a dream. Before long it felt as if we were truly meant for each other. As soon as he arrived home from work, we'd start chatting online until the early hours of the morning. We even picked out our children's names.

Whenever Marwan came to our house he would bring me presents from his trips to Lebanon, where he was working on a restoration project in Beirut. Sometimes he brought me a heavy Dior perfume or famous brands of make-up. One day he told me that he wanted to give me a piece of gold jewellery.

I plucked up my courage. '*Habibi*, this time can I choose my present?' I asked hesitantly.

'Finally!' Marwan replied. 'I'd given up asking you what you'd like. Tell me, my darling, what are you thinking of?'

'I'd like a necklace with a pendant engraved with verses from the Qur'an that are very special to me. Would you be able to do that?'

Of course Marwan said yes. And I told him how, many years ago, my uncle Abu Hamza had gathered his children and my kid brother, Adam, and me. He took out of his pocket folded-up pieces of paper with different verses from the Holy Qur'an. We each took one. My uncle told us that we had to look after our verses because there would come a day when they would be our means of survival. Mine were from Surah forty-one, Fussilat, verses thirty to thirty-two.

'Can I tell you something, but please don't judge me?' Marwan blushed. 'I don't even know them!'

And so I began: '*In the name of Allah, Most Gracious, Most Merciful.*' Then I recited the verses for him: '*As for those who say, "Our Lord is Allah", and who stand straight and steadfast, the angels descend on them, saying, "Fear not, nor grieve. But receive the good tidings of Paradise, which you were promised. We are your protectors in this life and in the Hereafter: therein you shall have all that your souls shall desire; therein you shall have all that you ask for. A hospitable gift from One Oft-Forgiving, Most Merciful.'"*

'Allah Almighty has spoken the truth,' Marwan exclaimed.

That night was magical. We were on Skype for hours, chatting about the Holy Qur'an and everything under the sun.

A few days later, Marwan returned from his trip with lots of presents. But not the necklace! Even though he had promised and even though I had asked for it myself!

I was too embarrassed to bring up the subject, but I kicked myself for telling him the story behind my special request. I regretted the fact that I had asked him to buy me something. But then I tried to convince myself that it was OK and that we learn from our mistakes. I had never asked anyone for anything in my whole life, not even my own father.

That evening, I didn't pick up when he rang. The next morning, I found dozens of missed calls and messages. I felt guilty and anxious and berated myself for the way I had reacted. Maybe he hadn't bought the necklace because he couldn't afford it, or maybe he'd simply forgotten. There were plenty of reasons and I shouldn't have responded in such a petty way.

The days dragged, and the month before the wedding felt like a year. I just couldn't wait to be with him.

*

'Congratulations, my darling,' Marwan said.

For the first time we were alone. Finally. My heart was racing. I was so scared, it was hard to believe how lively I had been just moments ago, dancing around the wedding hall.

'Congratulations to you too, and may Allah keep you by my side,' I replied.

As he walked towards me, I closed my eyes.

I felt him placing something around my neck.

'This is my wedding gift to you,' Marwan smiled proudly. 'They took a long time with the engraving because it needed a great deal of skill and precision to include all the verses. I didn't want to rush them so they would finish it well. And now here's the necklace you wanted. And for every baby you give me, I'll buy a gold lira engraved with the same verses for them.'

His vow meant the world to me. I looked at the pendant. The finish was indeed very professional and it was obvious that a lot of hard work had gone into it.

I threw my arms around my husband. 'May Allah help me make you even a quarter as happy as you've made me,' I exclaimed, my pendant sparkling as it caught the light.

I fell pregnant almost immediately. We started to plan how we would raise our children. Marwan couldn't wait for the birth of his first child. Suddenly, he wanted to protect me from the tiniest things. He even hired an Ethiopian housekeeper to make sure I didn't exert myself too much.

At first, all this was everything any woman would dream of. But soon it turned into a nightmare. Marwan would buy me books about pregnancy, babies and motherhood and forced me to read them because he wanted his child to be taken care of in the best possible way. Then we had to cut out all unhealthy food, which meant our meals became so bland I could barely eat them. We would rarely cook red meat, all fried and fatty foods were off the menu, and everything had to be steamed. And when the time came to find out the baby's gender, Marwan refused because he was worried about the evil eye if we discovered we were having a boy.

Life with Marwan became suffocating. I longed for the days when I used to go on leisurely strolls with my friends and nibble at pumpkin seeds. Gone were the days when I would laugh with them so hard we'd cry. We would buy falafel sandwiches and sit in the park to devour them, washed down with cans of Coca-Cola. These now-distant memories were far more special to me than dining at the fanciest restaurants. But I didn't breathe a word of this to Marwan.

I started to feel depressed and kept nagging him to let me go and visit my parents. I may have been exaggerating the situation, but I was missing them and my pregnancy was making me more tired than usual. Everything seemed a struggle. All I could talk about was how I wanted to go and see my family, even if only for a week, but Marwan refused to discuss the idea. When I was left with no other option, I called my mother-in-law and asked her to intervene. Otherwise, I threatened, I would go whether he liked it or not. I told her that I was suffering a great deal with my pregnancy and I needed someone from my family by my side. She gave me her word that she would talk to her son.

I was ironing in the bedroom when I heard Marwan opening the front door.

'*Habibti*,' he called out in a good mood. 'Where are you, my darling?'

'Here in the bedroom,' I replied. 'Come on in.'

'I have succumbed to you finally, my dear wife,' he said. 'Your wish is my command. Pack your bags, you will go to your family.' He placed the bus ticket on our bed.

I dropped the ironing. I was so excited.

'And you'll stay there until you give birth,' he added.

At this, my happiness evaporated.

'What's wrong with you, my darling?' he asked. 'Is there nothing that makes you happy?'

I shook my head. 'First you are overprotective and now you don't even want to be by my side when I give birth?'

Marwan walked towards me, sat me down on the bed and then settled next to me.

'Reham, *habibti*, you know that I can't wait for our child to be born. This is what I want more than anything else in the world. But my work is really busy at the moment and I can't afford to be careless, if only for the sake of this child. Now listen to what I'm going to say. No matter what I do, I won't be as helpful as your mother, right?'

'True,' I replied. 'But how can you…'

'Just be quiet for a second, stubborn one. Let me finish. As soon as you go into labour, I'll take some time off and come over right away.'

'Do you promise?' I asked.

'I promise.'

I travelled to my parents' home. Marwan sent money to cover my expenses and contacted me regularly to check I was well. My contractions started a couple of weeks early. At that point Marwan was in Lebanon. I asked my mother to call him as I went into hospital.

My labour was torture. But eventually I heard the sound of a baby crying and realized then that I had become a mother. The nurse congratulated me and told me that I had given birth to a beautiful baby girl. I smiled and fell into a deep, luxurious sleep.

The next day, I opened my eyes and Marwan was next to me, true to his word. My mother and everyone else were also in the room and the joy was palpable.

'Where's my daughter?' I asked.

My mother went to look for the nurse to bring the baby.

'My dear son,' my mother whispered to Marwan when she came back, 'please come with me. I need to talk to you.'

'What's wrong, Mama?' I asked.

'Nothing. They just want Marwan for something,' she replied.

'Who wants him?' I asked. 'Tell me, is there something wrong with my daughter?'

'Allah, help us. Allah is sufficient for us and He is the best of protectors.'

'What's wrong?' Marwan asked. 'Did something happen to the girl?'

'The girl...' my mother said. 'It turns out the girl has a disability.'

That word hit me like a thunderbolt. Suddenly, all the happiness I had felt was transformed into a torrent of tears as I doubled over, weeping. But what was worse was Marwan's reaction, which I will never forget.

'Disability?' he said. 'I will not have any disabled children. If that baby is disabled then we don't want anything to do with her.'

'What do you mean, you don't want her?' my mother asked. 'Don't let the devil get the better of you, my son.'

'When I say we don't want her, I mean it. And we won't take her.'

'What are you talking about?' I asked in disbelief. 'She's our daughter! What do you mean, we won't take her? Have you lost your mind, Marwan?'

Marwan didn't answer. Instead, he walked away, leaving me and our daughter behind. For three days I didn't hear a word from my husband. On the third day, he messaged me that he had to go back to Lebanon. He hadn't even laid eyes on his daughter once!

The doctors told me that my daughter had been born with Down's syndrome, which is still known in our culture as mongolism. But all I could see was my little angel with a smile as bright as the sun and a soul as pure as snow.

Still, I couldn't be happy after the way Marwan had reacted. The sorrow I felt dried up my milk and I couldn't breastfeed. Meanwhile, her father had disappeared into thin air.

My mother-in-law came to my parents' house to congratulate me on the birth and pierced the girl's ears, as is our custom. She promised to remind Marwan about the necklace he had said he would give the baby and I described to her how the lira pendant should be engraved with my verses from the Qur'an. When I asked her to also make sure he would register the baby, she sighed and begged me to be patient. I told her that we had agreed to name the baby Malaak, the Arabic for angel, if she was a girl, so he should register her under that name.

Two days later, my father-in-law came and told me that Marwan had asked him to register the baby.

'Did you register her as Malaak?' I asked him.

'No,' he replied. 'Marwan didn't agree to that and told me to name her Maya.'

'Maya!' My eyes widened in shock. 'Why?'

At first he tried to evade my question, but I insisted that he explain why my daughter hadn't been registered under the name we had chosen.

'Marwan said Malaak will be the name of his healthy daughter, not his disabled girl.' My father-in-law had lowered his gaze. 'He said he would call this one Maya because it's the name for a female monkey.'

I held my daughter in my arms. She was my little miracle. 'My darling,' I whispered to her. 'No matter what they call you, you will always be my angel. And I will never, ever let anyone harm you, my love.'

A whole month passed before Marwan called me. When I refused to speak to him, he started calling my family. He even enlisted the help of his parents to try to convince me to listen to him, claiming he had something urgent to talk to me about that he couldn't tell anyone else.

After some toing and froing and several heated arguments, my parents managed to persuade me to hear him out. They thought he must have seen the error of his ways and that he now wanted to meet his daughter. And the truth was, I missed him and didn't want my daughter to grow up without a father to lean on. I was ready to forgive him once again. It was stupid of me. Even then, deep inside me I knew I shouldn't have done that. But I did it anyway. That's the way for women in our culture: we spend our whole lives forgiving and getting nothing in return.

'You can't imagine how much I've missed you, Reham.' He had answered the phone straight away. 'The house feels so empty without you. I can't live without you. Everything reminds me of you.'

'Now you're telling me this?' I started, before remembering that I wanted to make things better, not worse. Softening my tone, I told him that I missed him too.

Neither of us said anything for the next few minutes as the sound of our breathing spoke a thousand words. It told tales of reproach, anguish, sadness and frustration. His voice made me forget everything he had done. It made me believe that he was truly sorry and I felt it was time to forgive and forget.

'Don't you want to come back to our home?' he asked.

'Of course I do, as soon as possible. I'm so tired,' I replied. 'I need to organize a few things for our daughter, though. Can you pick us up on Saturday?'

This time the silence was deafening. I couldn't even hear the sound of his breathing.

'Hello?' I asked. 'Where did you go? Did the line cut out?'

'That's not what we agreed,' Marwan eventually replied. 'Before I left, I told you that no daughter of mine is disabled.'

'What do you mean? I don't understand!'

'I mean that you will leave the girl at your parents' home, where they will raise her. Her expenses will be covered. They'll receive the money at the beginning of each month. Then we can finally forget all the pain we've suffered and we can go on to have normal children.'

'You want me to leave her?'

'Don't you dare even think of bringing that monkey with you.'

I hung up on him, switched my phone off, then stood up and started smashing everything around me in a frenzy. It wasn't long before my parents awoke and the baby started crying. As soon as I heard her, I felt something inside me soften. I kissed her and held her to my chest, singing and rocking her.

I awoke to my daughter's laughter, feeling exhausted. I tried to breastfeed her, once again without luck. So I prepared a bottle of formula instead. Playing with my baby helped ease my mind. A short while later, I went into the living room and dialled the number for Marwan's parents' house. My father-in-law replied.

'Hello, Uncle. How are you?' I started. 'Uncle, please, I want you to think of me as your own daughter. It wasn't that long ago that you all came over and made a huge fuss of me before taking me away from my parents' home, where I had been living like a queen. And now I am back at their home, being treated like a queen again. All that's left now is for the divorce papers to be sent to me. I'm willing to give up all my rights and I promise not to burden you with any responsibility towards my daughter.'

Marwan's father tried to convince me to change my mind, but I wouldn't budge. His wife tried too, but I stood my ground and told her I had nothing else to say.

'I'm sorry, but if he won't agree to an amicable divorce then I'll take him to court,' I said, before hanging up.

My family were standing around me, in shock.

'You want a divorce?' my mother asked. 'Are you mad? Do you want to make a laughing stock of us? What are we going to tell everyone? Oh, what will everyone think of us? *Ya Allah!*'

'My dear Reham,' my father started. 'My darling, don't listen to your mother. I know what kind of daughter I raised. And I trust your decisions. I will protect your daughter. I don't want to ever see you like you were yesterday, do you understand, my sweetheart?'

I hugged my father and wept as I felt the knot in my chest loosen. How I wished my daughter had a father like mine!

Marwan's family relayed our conversation to him, but he didn't believe that I had threatened to take him to the divorce court. When he called my parents' home, my father informed him that he no longer had a wife here. At this, Marwan lost his temper and started shouting at my father.

'Divorce?' he yelled. 'I'm not going to get divorced. My wife is coming back to her home.'

That night, my angel cried continuously and wouldn't stop. I had no idea what was wrong with her. I carried her around in my arms for hours.

Just before the dawn call to prayer with the first *Allahu Akbar, God is great*, my daughter suddenly fell silent. I had left Malaak on the bed while I performed my ablutions. I was about to pick her up to try and find out why she had suddenly stopped crying, when I heard the next part of the call: *Come to prayer! Come to success!* Smiling to myself, I thought it was an auspicious sign that she had stopped crying at the sound of the invitation to pray, and so I put on my prayer clothes and prayed.

Afterwards I wanted to move Malaak into her bed. But as soon as I picked her up, I could feel that her hands were ice cold. And her face had turned blue! I quickly loosened her clothes so I could check the rest of her body. Cold. Ice cold.

She had a smile on her face. Even until the moment she died, she had kept on smiling. She had arrived, stolen my soul, then left.

The doctors told me that she had died owing to a heart defect.

The shock was much more than I was able to bear. I locked myself in my room and isolated myself from everyone. I wept and wept, not only because I had lost my daughter, but because I felt I had betrayed her. I had promised to always protect her and never let anyone hurt her, but I hadn't been able to keep my promises. I couldn't even feed her with my own milk before she died. But pain and tears have never changed the course of fate. They have never been able to bring back someone dear or awaken the dead.

*

After that it was as though I had lost my mind. I sang and talked to my baby constantly, acting as though she were still with me. The next day, after Marwan heard the news, he travelled straight to Damascus and tried to visit, but my family refused to let him near me.

Three months passed and I remained in the same state. Marwan kept travelling back and forth in the hope of seeing me, but my father told him that nothing had changed and that I still wanted a divorce. Eventually, my mother convinced me to put the past behind us, saying that my condition was deteriorating and that they had to save me or else they would lose their daughter too. She reasoned that, despite everything that had happened, my husband still wanted me and hadn't abandoned me. And so my parents decided to invite Marwan over for dinner.

When he arrived with his parents, my mother told me to go out and greet him. Before I reached them, I heard their voices. And I immediately recalled Malaak's smile. I had never seen a baby laugh the way she did. And then I remembered her cold body in my arms. It all came rushing back to me: how she wasn't breathing or moving. I began to cry and slapped my face and shouted, 'That bastard has to die! He has to die!' And I threatened to kill Marwan with my bare hands if I ever had to lay eyes on him again. Of course Marwan could hear me, since I was screaming at the top of my voice. He left and I was told he travelled again a short while later.

*

My uncle Abu Hamza came over to see me.

'Your parents are worried about you,' Abu Hamza said. 'How long are you going to go on like this?'

'Until Allah improves the situation, until He relieves matters.'

I will never forget how my uncle looked down for five whole minutes, holding his prayer beads. Suddenly, I heard the beautiful sound of his voice as he recited my verses of the Qur'an.

'*In the name of Allah, Most Gracious, Most Merciful. As for those who say, "Our Lord is Allah," and stand straight and steadfast, the angels descend on them, saying, "Fear not, nor grieve. But receive the good tidings of Paradise, which you were promised. We are your protectors in this life and in the Hereafter: therein you shall have all that your souls shall desire; therein you shall have all that you ask for. A hospitable gift from One Oft-Forgiving, Most Merciful."*'

My heart began to pound. He repeated it. Tears were pouring from my eyes. His voice was so beautiful and warm.

'Recite it again,' I pleaded.

'My daughter,' he said, 'the Qur'an was revealed so that we would consider its meaning and let it help us solve the matters of our life. Consider the meaning of these verses so that you can emerge from this crisis. May Allah bless you with happiness and contentment.'

'How?' I asked him. 'I'm so tired. And it feels like I'm losing my mind.'

'*As for those who say, "Our Lord is Allah!"*' he repeated.

'*There is no God but Allah and Muhammad is His prophet*,' I said.

'*And stand straight and steadfast.*'

'I don't understand,' I said.

'When He gave, you were content, but when He took…'

I remained silent, not uttering a single word.

'I was also content,' I finally said, quietly.

'Are you sure, my daughter?' he asked.

He walked away, leaving me alone with the holy verses hanging over me and his voice, which lingered in my mind. His last question echoed in my head: *Are you sure, my daughter?*

I spent the next week quietly and calmly contemplating what I should do, and considering my life in a rational manner, the way anyone thinks about their future and dreams.

Then I packed my bag and said a little prayer, asking Allah to help guide me along the right path so that I wouldn't regret my decision later.

As soon as I saw Marwan, I could smell Malaak and I had to turn away.

'Are you still upset with me?' he asked.

I shook my head silently.

Our home was exactly the same as it was when I left, even though I'd been gone for eight months. Everything was in its place: my clothes were hanging in exactly the same way in my wardrobe, the bed linen was folded away in the same cupboards and the furniture was in exactly the same place.

Marwan had prepared a meal for us. I can't remember what we chatted about. All I remember is that I tried to avoid eye contact as much as possible.

While I was doing the washing-up, I suddenly felt him near me, trying to get closer. The plate I was holding dropped and smashed on the floor. Marwan asked me not to move in case I hurt myself and said he would clear it up. I walked out of the kitchen, leaving him there, my heart pounding. When he'd finished, he came and found me sitting in the living room.

'My darling, didn't you miss me?' he asked.

'Yes, I did,' I lied.

Youssef's Kingdom

'That's enough. Enough,' he says. 'Every day you cry and go on and on about this. You're going to torture yourself to death, and kill me with you. What kind of a fucking life is this? Let it go.'

'I want a child,' she cries, 'to play with, to love, and who'll love me back. A kid I can feed with my own hands. I want to spoil him and buy him the best clothes and toys there are. I want to carry him in my arms and feel how he fills my whole world with joy.'

'You've been saying the same thing for years now,' he shouts. 'You can't have children. Wake up, for God's sake.'

Then, all of a sudden, he calms down. He has had an idea about how to make his wife happy and increase his wealth and power in the camp at the same time. He's had this idea for a while. It's time to make it happen.

'You are kind and caring,' he now says gently to his wife, sitting down on the bed next to her, stroking the hair away from her face. 'And you are right. You are so good with children. Children trust you. That's a blessing that should not go to waste. Children help us and make things easier for us. And all it takes is a sweetie or a cigarette and they'll be yours. They'll be in the palms of your hands to mould as you please. What more do we want?'

That wicked Youssef, tall, broad-shouldered and tattooed all over like the wrestlers on TV. His hair's long and he's got a thick, black beard. He has a certain reputation – wears a gun round his waist, even when he sleeps. He knows no mercy and has no friends – that is, until he needs something. That's how he lives his life. He grew up on the streets in the camp and he's memorized every inch of the place. He's notorious even beyond the camp, a thug. But no law can touch him because the police never enter Shatila. He owns a small coffee shop, a space for all his wheeling and dealing. He married Samar not out of any love or passion, or those stories of Antar and Abla and Majnun and Layla. No. He needed a wife. For the bed. And now, he knows, for business too.

Youssef grips his shisha pipe, takes a deep drag and blows out more and more smoke, his eyes lost in the fog, imagining the shapes of dreams which he sketches with every breath he takes from his hubble-bubble.

Youths gather in his coffee shop. Shisha, coffee, iced tea and the other things that come out late at night: hashish, pills, alcohol, plus gambling. Youssef supervises everything and cheats everyone. That's his way: deceit-ful and untrustworthy, like a sly fox. A con artist who manipulates people until he gets what he wants, takes what he needs from them before shoving them head first into the first rubbish bin he comes across.

He takes another drag. His new plan is good. And he's managed to persuade Samar. She'll have some kids to look after.

A sound like an explosion rips through the air. Calmly, Youssef puts his pipe down on the small table. No one is disturbed by the sound. Even the *ful* bean seller with his cart does not break stride.

'Who hasn't paid?' Youssef shouts.

One of the electricity boxes he owns has just fused, meaning that someone in the neighbourhood has not paid their bill.

'Yeah, Chief, I should have mentioned.' Muneef, the boy he employs in the café, now stands in front of him with an apologetic grin on his ugly face. 'There's still Ahmad's apartment on the second floor. The apartment that's near the stairs. Says he hasn't got enough money to feed his own family. Says if you wait a few days he'll be able to pay you back.'

Youssef turns red in the face. 'Are we running a fucking guest house or what? Go and fetch that little piece of shit right away!'

'As Allah is my witness, Chief Youssef, I haven't a penny to my name. I have nothing. I'm living on the breadline. I don't have any money. My life is in your hands.'

Ahmad stands in front of Youssef, bowed head, hands shaking.

Pathetic! Youssef draws out his gun from the back of his trousers.

'Tomorrow you have the money or else.' He raises the gun towards the sky and fires a shot.

Ahmad has shut his eyes in fear. He has no idea where he will get the money. He spent his final pennies here in the café last night.

He opens his eyes again. But Youssef has already lost interest. His phone is ringing. As he pulls it out of his pocket, he impatiently waves Ahmad away.

'My man, yes, that's why I've been trying to get hold of you. Didn't I tell you I'd call you? You're always in a rush. But anyway, I've got another idea to make sure we don't get our hands dirty. Listen, I have a few kids here who beg on the street. Syrians mainly.

'Samar has got close to them. They do what she tells them to now. They wipe windscreens at traffic lights in a classy neighbourhood where no one gives them a second glance. I want you to take them and train them, OK? And explain to them exactly what's needed from them and how, if anything happens and they're arrested, then no one is to say a word. Frighten them, threaten them, that's your job.

'Yeah, that sounds like an excellent plan.

'Don't worry, Samar's got them under control. She's good with kids. Didn't I tell you that these kids are begging at the traffic lights and on the streets and alleys?

'Yeah, there is Hamouda – thirteen, a mongol. He'll finish off the jobs for us without anyone suspecting him. And that other kid, Mansour, ten years old, he's thin and light-footed and he's got a very slim hand. He's a little pickpocket, so keep an eye on your wallet and all that. And then there's Faid, the gang leader. Fourteen and he's the one managing them. He sends them off to different streets and also protects them from the other kids since he's big and broad. Their families don't care, too tired, too busy trying to muster what little food, drink and rent they can. This world has left them dizzy. Mothers running after a morsel of bread so that they can survive, and looking for some sort of security and stability. And in the meantime they have lost their children to the Shatila alleyways. I play father to the poor bastards. Samar loves it. As for their real fathers, we shouldn't worry. Most of them don't even know where their fathers are and whether they're in this world or the next. Some are missing, some have been killed, some detained. Some emigrated and no one knows where they've gone or whether they've been swallowed up by the sea…' He pauses before adding very slowly, 'And some are simply too poor to say no to me.'

At this point Youssef suddenly turns and looks Ahmad straight in the eyes. Ahmad cowers under his gaze. He'd thought Youssef had forgotten all about him. But he now realizes that the other man had been aware of him eavesdropping all the while. And that Youssef's last sentence was meant for him.

The White Dress

As Jafra sways from side to side, so too does her dress.
The short, purple frock was a gift from her father for
her ninth birthday, two years ago. Even though it's a
bit tight now she still feels pretty in it. The girl begins
dancing through the room, clutching the doll in her arms
closer to her chest. She hums along with the song that is
blaring out from the old wooden radio, while the doll's
long black hair swings to and fro to the rhythm of the
music. Jafra is named after the martyred hero celebrated
in this song. A symbol of the Palestinian cause and a
source of great pride, Jafra, the fearless revolutionary
Palestinian fighter who was killed in an Israeli air strike
over Beirut in 1976, is a national icon. Many poems and
songs have been inspired by her.

The girl turns the radio off. The apartment falls silent
again. Her parents are out: her mother at work at the
sewing workshop, and her father probably at the café,
where he spends most of his time. Sitting down on the
green rug, Jafra sorts through the scraps of different-
coloured and textured cloth her mother always brings
back from the workshop. Today she wants to make a

new dress for her doll. Purple would of course be nice. Matching her own dress. But there are no purple scraps. There are quite a few white lacy ones, though. Jafra fishes them out from the heap and holds the lace against her dress. Yes, white lace and purple go well together. The vibrant combination puts a smile on her face.

Jafra threads yarn into a needle and begins to work on her doll's new dress. With her black hair, Rita will look so beautiful in white. Jafra would love to have a white lacy dress herself one day too. She will ask her mother if she can bring more scraps home. And maybe, if she gets lots, then Jafra could also sew a new dress for her mum. But a colourful one. To put a smile back on her lips. She so rarely smiles nowadays, especially since her husband's illness has got much worse.

Jafra can still remember her parents being happy, laughing and joking. They married against their families' wishes, her father once told her. 'Your mother was just too beautiful to let her slip away,' he said, with a twinkle in his eye. Jafra's mum comes from an uneducated peasant family that arrived in Shatila from the Palestinian village of Sha'at, whereas her dad's family are town folk from Haifa, and they used to be rich when they still lived in their homeland. After they married, Jafra's father dreamed of having a son whom he would call George, after George Habash, the founder of the Popular Front for the Liberation of Palestine. But Jafra's mother would have called the boy Ammar, the nickname of Yassar Arafat from the Fatah movement. So, for a long time, Jafra believed it was lucky that they only had her, a girl. Now her father suffers from depression. He needs lots of medicine, and the alcohol and all the drugs are 'messing with his head', her mother says.

Jafra looks up. The room is almost dark. She has forgotten the time, so engrossed has she been in her work. And her mum isn't back yet! Suddenly Jafra's entire body begins to tremble. Mum is late! And today she promised to be home early because it's payday and she said that she would buy Jafra a toffee apple. Why is she late? Jafra hates being alone with her dad, and he always comes back once it gets dark, demanding his supper. And if he sees there is no supper, he will be angry and then fall into a rage and beat her because Mum isn't around.

'It's because he feels powerless and out of control,' her mother says.

'It's because he's not allowed to work outside the camp,' her mother says.

The wounds on Jafra's back from the last beating are still raw.

The girl hears the front door opening. Her fingers twirl her hair as she frantically tries to think of a plan within the next few seconds. But she can't think, she's too scared.

Quickly, she lies down on the green rug next to her doll and closes her eyes. Hopefully her dad will think she's asleep and let her be.

The door opens. One person shuffles in. Then another. The girl holds her breath, squeezing her eyes tight.

'How much did you earn this week?' Her father's voice.

'Fifty thousand,' her mother replies. Jafra is about to jump up with relief, but then her mother continues: 'But please don't take it all. I want to pay Abu Mahmoud, the grocer, back. We've owed him money for four months now and haven't yet repaid a single lira.'

'Don't worry, *habibti*, my darling.' Her father's voice sounds soft. 'I don't want the money. I have enough. And I've sorted Abu Mahmoud. The debt has been paid off and we don't owe him anything now. Keep the money and tomorrow I want you to go to Sabra market to buy a white dress for Jafra, a long one preferably, since she's not a little girl any more. She's almost a woman. But don't be back late. Make sure you'll have enough time to cook a feast, because Abu Mahmoud is coming over for dinner.'

A new dress! A white one! Her father knows what she, Jafra, is thinking. Like he used to. 'I can read your mind through walls,' he'd tell her. Jafra opens her eyes, sits up, but at that moment she sees her father playfully pulling her mother into the bedroom. Her mother laughs. Maybe everything will turn out fine after all. The door closes behind her parents. With a warm feeling in her tummy, Jafra lies back down again.

At some point she feels her mother gently waking her up, leading her to her bed, undressing her and tucking her under the duvet.

*

When Jafra wakes, her parents are still asleep. Like every morning, she examines her pillow closely. Her father yanks at her hair whenever he beats her. In places it has become so fragile that it often falls out overnight, like the leaves of the trees in autumn when they turn yellow and drop. Even now, Jafra finds a strand of her hair. She twists it into a small ball, suddenly remembering what she overheard last night. Did she really hear it, or was it just a beautiful dream?

Tiptoeing over to her parents' bedroom, she prays that her dad is still asleep. She stands by the doorway, takes a deep breath, then pokes her head in slightly to take a quick look. Once she can see that he's asleep, she relaxes. She wakes her mother with a little kiss and with a nod of her head asks her silently to follow her outside the room.

'Last night I dreamed I would get a new dress,' she whispers as soon as they are in the kitchen.

'No, it wasn't a dream,' her mother says, laughing.

Not long afterwards, Jafra is unlocking the front door.

'Hurry up, Mama, hurry up! We don't have much time. We're going to be late!'

She tears at her mother's hand, then charges off, her head turning every which way, as if she doesn't want to waste a single opportunity to look at the things they chance upon. The girl scrutinizes everything around her as if she's seeing it for the first time. She wants to remember this beautiful day in minute detail. When she spots chalk marks on the ground in front of one of her friends' houses, her face lights up.

'Uncle Jihad's kids must have been playing *hajla*. Please, Mama, I want to see them. I haven't visited Mais and Khadijah in so long. Please, we won't be late. Just for half an hour or so. And you can drink coffee with Um Khadijah.'

Of course, what Jafra really wants to do is to tell her friends about the white dress they are about to buy.

Her mother hesitates for a moment but then agrees. It's nice to be out with her daughter and she'll make sure that they return in good time to cook the dinner.

Um Khadijah and her daughters are thrilled to see their guests. The two women drink coffee and share a shisha, the girls drink lemonade.

'Stay for some food, Um Jafra,' Um Khadijah says with a sigh. 'We have so much to catch up on.'

'I wish I could,' Jafra's mother replies. 'But I promised Jafra that we would go to the market to buy her a new white dress.'

Jafra hasn't yet mentioned her new dress to her friends. She suddenly feels embarrassed.

'And we're already late,' her mother adds. 'I have a big meal to prepare. Abu Mahmoud, the grocer, is coming over for dinner. And you know what Ahmad is like and what he'll do if I'm home late.'

'Oh, Jafra, you're in luck,' Um Khadijah exclaims, clapping her hands together like an excited child.

'I bought Mais a white dress yesterday. It was reduced in the market. She needs something nice for her uncle Khaled's wedding. But –' and Um Khadijah pretends to slap her own cheeks as if a catastrophe has descended upon them – 'the dress for Mais! It's far too small for my daughter. It would suit someone slimmer, like you, Jafra.'

The dress Um Khadijah now fetches is blindingly beautiful. Lace and sparkles and ribbons, much nicer than what Jafra could ever have sewn. Much nicer than Rita's dress. Much nicer than her mother could have afforded to buy. Jafra and her mother stay for food and the women's and girls' laughter can be heard up and down the narrow alleyway.

Adam

I throw back the shutters to let in some fresh air and immediately find myself facing another window, less than a metre away. The window belongs to an apartment in the building next door.

'*Ya Allah*, please let this home be a blessing for us,' I sigh.

Marwan, my sister Reham's husband, has found us this place with his connections here in Shatila. And finally we have been able to move in.

Through the open window, I can see a sofa, a table and the glare of a TV screen, but there is no one in sight, even though the television is on.

The news reporter on the Palestinian channel is talking about the 'electricity crisis' in the Shatila camp, which, she explains, 'lies in the heart of the Lebanese capital, Beirut'.

'For over five years, the Palestinians here have been suffering due to a multitude of problems related to the electricity supply and the almost daily outage, leaving some families without any power for days on end. The accumulation of electrical cables, often entangled with numerous water pipes less than two metres off the ground, has turned the camp into a series of terrifyingly chaotic alleys, half of which are too narrow to allow two people to pass through. And so the problem – no, the crisis – emerges of phantom currents, as many of the structures have become live.'

A boy, roughly my age, has suddenly appeared and now switches off the television. He turns. I recognize him. It's Muneef, who met us on the first day. I'm about to smile, greet him. But something in his hostile, fixed gaze holds me back.

'Oh, come on,' he then scoffs, dismissively jilting his head backwards. 'Don't tell me these Syrians have now moved in next door. That's all we need.'

I quietly close the shutters and turn around to find both my parents standing behind me, having seen and heard everything. My mother gives me a hug.

'Don't let it get to you, son.' My father pats my back. 'Just ignore him. There are a lot of screwed-up people out there.'

I nod, but my mind is racing. Since when has 'Syrian' become a dirty word? Aren't we all Palestinians here? What a racist idiot!

As the sun begins to set, I decide to go out for a walk. I change into a fresh pair of jeans and a black T-shirt. Then I wrap my keffiyeh around my neck, an outward symbol of my own Palestinian heritage.

For a while I walk aimlessly through the narrow alleys and streets, until I hear drumming and a general din. A wedding celebration. A crowd in formal suits and dresses has gathered to celebrate with the bride and groom. Everyone is singing and dancing to the beat of the wedding band, who are all dressed in elegant white outfits. I stop nearby, feeling the band's rhythm in my blood.

Suddenly, two young men appear brandishing rifles and silver revolvers in holsters around their hips. It seems they are friends of the groom, as they wave and then start firing bullets into the air joyously. The guests continue to dance, clearly unperturbed, while I am very aware that my heart is racing and the palms of my hands have turned sweaty. The two men continue emptying their ammunition into the air. Shell casings litter the street.

For the next two weeks, I hole myself up within the four walls of our apartment. I even avoid opening the shutters of my bedroom window so I don't run the risk of being verbally assaulted by the idiot from the other side. My lack of friends and loneliness are overwhelming. And as my desperation grows, the more I feel I am being buried alive. Or bricked in. The buildings around me grow higher by the day, unsafe and unregulated, in an attempt to provide shelter for an ever larger number of refugees flooding in from all over Syria. And often when I wake up the sky appears smaller than the previous day.

'*Habibi* Adam,' my mother says to me one evening. 'You need to go back to school and finish your final year. It's the best you can do at the moment. School starts next week.' Then she adds, 'Don't worry. The school is run by UNRWA, which means all the students are Palestinian and from the camp.'

I nod, but I have no desire to do anything at all, let alone go to a school full of people I don't know. What do I know about Lebanon? Maybe they'll all be as bigoted as that guy Muneef next door!

All of the students in my class are Palestinian. Some are Lebanese Palestinians, while others, like me, are Palestinians who have fled the war in Syria. The class is divided into two, with the female students sitting on the left and the boys on the right, and a male and a female teacher. I sit there completely silent, until the student next to me asks about my age, what my name is and where I live. The rest of the day I spend making random acquaintances.

A few days later, as I stand during break time with a group of boys from my class, I spot a tall boy staggering towards me, followed by a gang of about twenty. I immediately recognize him as the bully from next door, Muneef. He stops and squares his shoulders, then raises his hand and pats me patronizingly on the shoulder.

'What's up, Syrian?' he sneers.

I shove him and his friends pounce on us. The school-yard turns into a battlefield until the clash eventually lands us all in the headmaster's office.

*

That afternoon I stagger back to the camp, tired and depressed, having spoken barely two words since we were released from the headmaster's office. I'm walking fast, keeping my head low, but my eyes are restlessly scanning the path. I want to avoid encountering anyone from school, especially my neighbour. All I want is to get back to our apartment as quickly as possible and hide in bed for the rest of the day.

Suddenly I feel a soft splat on my head and then something wet running down my forehead. Pigeon shit! It happens a lot in the camp and it always surprises me how, with all these wires running over our heads, the bird shit still gets through. Like a ghost of a long-gone past, a memory of myself back home, back in Yarmouk, passes through my mind. In Yarmouk I would have laughed out loud with my friends about that pigeon shit running down my forehead and now dripping onto my shirt. But here in Shatila, in this moment, I want to cry like a baby. As if even the pigeons are poking fun at me, insulting me, hate me being here. Off to my left I notice a tiny alley with no one in it. With my bare hands I rub my face and my shirt as clean as possible, then I wipe my hands on my trousers. There is still no one in the alley. I take that chance and for a moment I lean against the wall, closing my eyes, finding my bearings again.

The sound of a *nay* is wafting towards me. I open my eyes again. It's coming from an open window somewhere above me. I recognize the melody of one of my favourite songs, 'The Breeze is upon Us', by Fairuz, 'the First Lady of Lebanese singing'. Pressing my head against the wall again, I strain to catch the beautiful melody. The sublime sound tugs at my heart and I can't control myself any longer. For the first time since we have left home, I start singing out loud, my voice rising and rising, my heart becoming lighter and lighter, I don't care if anyone hears me, until I'm belting the song out with my mouth wide open:

'A breeze passes over us
from the fork in the valley.
O breeze, for the sake of love
take me home.

'O breeze,
Take my love with you.
There's a wallflower,
a small window and a photograph.
O breeze, take me to them.'

Suddenly, the music stops and my voice is shocked into silence. A man's face is looking down on me. I turn to walk away.

'Wait!' he calls after me. 'Was it you singing?'

For a moment I hesitate. I should perhaps just walk on. But I stop. If people are rude to me, I still don't have to be rude to them.

'Yes.' I turn my face upwards to look at the man.

'Your voice is amazing,' the man says with an open smile.

'Thank you.' I feel myself relaxing.

'Do you have a moment? Come up here. We need a singer.'

He must have noticed my brief delay in replying because he adds, 'This is a public cultural centre. Anyone from the camp can use it.'

As I climb the stairs, I spot a toilet. Over the sink I rinse my face and wash away the last of the bird excrement from my hands. They are now clean and no longer smell.

The man is in his early thirties and introduces himself as Ghasif. With him is a young woman, Shatha. I'm guessing she must be two or three years older than me. It's her who's holding the *nay*.

'I'm just the teacher,' Ghasif says, laughing as he sees me looking at the *nay* in Shatha's hand. 'There's a talent show here in a few weeks' time. I'm helping the musicians to train for it. Shatha and I agree that it would be wonderful if she could accompany a singer.'

'It's difficult to find good singers,' Shatha now says, though she's too shy to look me in the eyes. 'I couldn't believe it when I heard someone singing downstairs.'

'Thank you,' I reply, blushing. 'And you play beautifully.' She now lifts her gaze with a smile. Encouraged, I continue: 'That was the first time I've ever sung out loud, by the way. You're the first people ever to hear me sing. I never sing in front of anyone.'

'Oh, but that's not right,' Ghasif exclaims. 'Someone like you should be singing to a large audience. Honestly, you've got an incredible voice. Do you have time to join us?'

I nod, slightly overwhelmed by the sudden turn of events.

'Then let's get things going.' Enthusiastically Ghasif claps his hands.

Shatha starts to play and I follow her fingers as they move along the *nay* until I find myself lost in another world, drowning in the melodic waves that tease my soul. As soon as I recognize the song by Um Kulthoum, I join in.

> *'Your eyes took me back*
> *to days gone by.*
> *They taught me to regret*
> *the past and its wounds.'*

As Shatha plays, Ghasif signals with one hand for me to raise my voice. My voice trembles, since this is the first time I have sung in front of someone who is actually listening to me. I straighten up, breathe more deeply, with every note, with every word, becoming steadier and gaining in confidence.

> *'Whatever I saw*
> *before my eyes saw you*
> *is wasted.*

How could they count it
as part of my life?
You are my life.'

I carry on singing, lost in the moment until we naturally begin to slow down, exhausted but elated. I haven't felt that motivated and happy for a long time.

Over the following weeks, we meet every afternoon. Often around five o'clock, because Shatha has a job in a drug rehabilitation centre just outside the camp on the other side. Most of the time Shatha and I practise on our own. Sometimes we chat – about music and books. I write the lyrics to a song in the Palestinian dialect and she composes the music.

'Palestine calls to the breeze:
"Won't you bring something back for me?
A little of the air they breathe
from the camp where my family are refugees?"'

It is only on the morning of the show that the thought suddenly crosses my mind that after today Shatha and I won't have a reason to meet any longer. For a while this realization presses me down onto my bed. Then I decide that the best way of ensuring that we continue to make music together is to not disappoint her today, to give my best performance ever.

The challenge energizes me and I feel adrenalin

coursing through my veins. I jump out of bed and run gel through my hair, which I never normally do, and style it painstakingly. Shooting a quick glance at myself in the mirror, I then smile and blow a kiss at the handsome young man looking back at me. I hear giggling behind me. My sister, Reham, who's come to our apartment to walk with my parents to the cultural centre to hear me perform, blows me a kiss. I grab a pillow and throw it at her.

As I walk out of the building I quickly glance up at Muneef's apartment. Ever since the talk in the headmaster's office we've been avoiding each other. I turn the corner and, before I can hold my breath, close off my senses, the smell of an open sewage drain assaults me. I speed up, but the smell infiltrates my airways, lungs and brain cells. Words cannot describe the overwhelming stench of putrefaction and decay that wafts up from these overloaded drains. No respectful words at least. Stepping over this one, I hold my breath until I'm several metres away. My lungs emit a sound as if a cat has been strangled. My pulse quickens and I cough so much that I am red in the face. Then regular air flows back into my body. I straighten up, and over my shoulder I cast a triumphant look at the open sewer, as if I have just won a battle. I smile at my own silliness.

I'm about to look forward again, when I accidentally bump into an elderly woman. Before I can apologize, she screeches, 'You're the one! You're the one who killed them! You're the one who killed them!'

I stand frozen to the spot. In the meantime, she bends down, takes off one of her shoes and raises it, falling back against the side of the building.

'You murderer! Murderer!'

Footsteps are racing towards us and Shatha rushes over, takes the old woman by the hand and talks to her gently until she walks away.

'Are you OK?' Shatha's concerned face is close to mine. I nod.

'Poor woman,' Shatha says quietly as we continue on our way together. 'She's not in her right mind. She saw her entire family – husband, parents, siblings and three of her own children – murdered during the Sabra and Shatila massacre. Only one daughter survived, Latifa, who was a baby back then.'

For a moment we walk on quietly. I'm searching for something to say but I can't think of anything.

'Latifa married my uncle Ahmad, the brother of my late mother,' Shatha continues. 'But he's not a good man. Lots of drugs and alcohol from an early age. But Latifa loves him, while her mother, the old woman you've just met, hates him. And so she hasn't talked to her daughter in years. Says she lost all her children in the massacre.'

Abruptly Shatha falls silent. I throw a side-glance at her and see that she's lost in thought. Then she shakes her head as if talking to herself, turns her face towards me and flashes me one of her charming smiles.

'Let's hurry. We don't want to be late for our own show.'

There are fifteen acts including ours, all to be performed on a large stage set up on the roof of the centre. First is a theatrical performance, which is followed by a boy rapping. All too quickly, our names are called and I real-ize that my hands are trembling. I look at Shatha and can see that she too is nervous. Her left eye is twitching. Recognizing her tension somehow helps to alleviate mine, and as soon as we walk onto the stage I forget about my sweaty brow and clammy hands.

Shatha sits down on a chair and starts to play a gentle melody to an immediately captivated audience. I stand by the microphone. The second I start singing, the audi-ence – made up of the other performers, their families and friends, and workers from the centre – begin to roar with excitement. I see the proud faces of my parents beaming in the third row, right in the middle. A burst of love and warmth emanates from the crowd, with the sound of their applause rising so high it threatens to drown us out. Glancing over at Shatha, I can see that she too has picked up on the amazing vibe.

After the end of the show, we stand alongside the other artists on stage next to the judging panel. One of the panel members strides over to the microphone.

'We are thrilled to announce that the winners of today's talent show are... Shatha and Adam!'

Shatha and I lock eyes.

Then I start leaping into the air, buoyed up by the seemingly endless applause. Reeling with joy, Shatha and I sway towards the judges side by side. I'm aware that my upper arm brushes hers a couple of times. The panel begin to confer our award and hand each of us a special plaque. We have our photo taken with the awards and then step off the stage, only to be set upon by the audience, who surround us, their cameras flashing.

'Quiet, please! Can we have some quiet, please!' someone shouts through the microphone, and everyone falls silent.

'The ceremony is not quite over,' the unfamiliar voice continues. 'I am a friend of the centre. Some of you may know me as Mr Hadi. I was so impressed by the winning performance that I have decided to bestow an additional gift on the winners: I pledge to finance the recording of that wonderful song and to distribute it to all the Palestinian and Lebanese radio stations.'

Everyone in the audience erupts in applause and more cheering.

When Shatha's and my hands touch briefly as the crowd encircles us once more, her energy enters through my fingertips, rushes up my arm and into my body like an electric current.

The Dinner

Latifa is worried. She and Jafra are late getting back. How will she explain their delay to Ahmad? She should have left sooner, not stayed for food and then another shisha at Um Khadijah's. Now Ahmad will be angry and might have even nipped down to the café. The drinking is a curse. He used to be so smart, but his brain is disintegrating. Hopefully the fact that she's coming back with more money than expected will appease him. It means they can pay their electricity bill.

'And where have you been?'

As soon as Latifa opens the door, Ahmad's voice hits them square in the face. He must have been waiting behind the door. But Latifa can't smell any alcohol on his breath. Which is good news. Maybe he has held himself back because of Abu Mahmoud's visit. Abu Mahmoud is a pious man and disapproves of any intoxicating substances. Still, Latifa pushes Jafra into her room, out of the way and into safety. Then she heads for the kitchen. Ahmad follows her. She unpacks the shopping bag.

'Dinner will be ready in half an hour. Abu Mahmoud will enjoy a feast.' She takes out the money. 'I only spent 5,000 liras on vegetables for the dinner. The dress didn't cost me anything.' She explains what has happened.

For a few seconds Ahmad just stares at the banknotes in his wife's hands. Then he grabs them and stuffs them into his trouser pockets. He turns on his heels and walks out.

Abu Mahmoud arrives right on time, leaning on his cane. The old man is short and chubby, with a belly as big as that of a heavily pregnant woman. He's in traditional Palestinian dress: a black-and-white striped *qumbaz* robe, his bald head hidden under a *hatta* head-dress and cord. He used to have two wives but both have died, leaving him with eleven children and many grandchildren, he can't remember how many. When he wants to see a grandchild he calls out all the names under the sun and then at least one of them comes running up to him.

Ahmad greets his guest warmly and kisses him on his forehead, as a mark of respect. In the kitchen he tells Latifa to fetch Jafra from her room and to make sure she's wearing clean clothes.

'I want her to make a good impression. And the smile should never leave your face or hers.'

An awkward silence hangs over their dinner, which Latifa attempts to break.

'I have heard from the women in the workshop that you're looking for a bride to...'

But the sound of Jafra bursting into laughter interrupts her mother's question as the girl splutters and almost spits out her food. Shooting her daughter an angry look from across the table, Latifa notices Ahmad, who is obviously on edge, his face flushed and covered in small beads of sweat.

Abu Mahmoud turns to Ahmad. 'Yes, that's true,' he says, smiling slyly. 'And I've found my bride.'

After dinner, with his tea in his hands, the old man spends the rest of the evening boasting about his achievements and how much money he makes.

This evening Ahmad does not go to the café, not even once Abu Mahmoud has left. After Latifa has cleared the table and finished the washing-up, he pats the place next to him on the sofa.

'Come and sit with me. I need to tell you something. I've given Abu Mahmoud my blessing to marry Jafra. Their wedding will be on Thursday.'

Latifa feels her head begin to turn. From one side to the other. And back. As the meaning of her husband's last two sentences sink in. And the awful truth is that somehow what she has just heard doesn't surprise her. There were a couple of fleeting moments during the day when fear had gripped her heart. Each time she knew for a split second that it had to do with the white dress for Jafra and Abu Mahmoud coming for dinner. But the thought had been too implausible to let it develop fully in her head. Ahmad would never do such a thing. There are other men in the camp who would, but not Ahmad. Not her husband, whom she married for love.

Latifa now opens her mouth and begins to scream and to drum her fists against her husband's chest, then beats her own face with her palms, then hits Ahmad again. Ahmad does not react. He sits motionless, waiting for the storm to subside.

Waking up to the sound of her mother's wails, Jafra silently starts to cry. Assuming that her father is once again drunk and beating her mother as usual, she's too frightened to come out from under her blanket in case her father might turn on her.

Later that night, Latifa sneaks into her daughter's room and climbs into her bed, trying not to wake her. She just wants to lie next to her baby and listen to her breathing.

'I had no choice,' Ahmad said. 'Our debts have mounted. We need a whole year's income just to pay back what we owe for bread alone. I can't work outside the camp. You know that. We have no work permit. We have no status. I'm no one.'

His voice was trembling. Latifa looked at her husband in disbelief. Contempt.

'Everyone is in the same situation,' she hissed. She wanted to spit at him. She hated to see her strong husband acting so weak.

'Tell me! What could I do that I haven't already done? I can't even buy the medication I'm supposed to take every day because we're trying to repay our debts. And your wage isn't enough... it barely covers half the month's expenses and the other half we cover through loans. And we have to pay the rent at the beginning of next month, otherwise they'll throw us out on the street. Say something! Why aren't you saying anything?'

He was crying now, wailing like an old woman. And it was her, Latifa, who sat motionless, speechless, numb like a piece of rock. Then the words shot out of her mouth before she could hold them back.

'You are inhuman. You're sacrificing your daughter, selling her to an old man, like a piece of cattle.' She didn't know where she found the courage. She had never spoken to her husband like this before. 'It's all your fault. The drinking. The gambling.' She raised both hands to her mouth. He would hit her now. Beat her to death. She had gone too far.

But tonight Ahmad didn't beat her. 'It's not as you think,' he sobbed. 'Abu Mahmoud just wants someone to look after him, like a nurse. His eyesight is getting weaker, he needs someone to help him out of bed in the morning. He won't... he won't touch her.'

Ahmad tried to grab Latifa's hands, but she pulled them away from him. He bent forward, pressing his arms against his stomach as if in pain. Then suddenly his upper body rose up again.

'I'm trying to save our daughter,' he said, calmer, in control once more. 'A couple of days ago Youssef threatened me because we hadn't paid our electricity bill. I knew and he knew it wasn't just because of the electricity. I have... I had gambling debts with him. He threatened me with a gun. But he wouldn't kill me. Of course. I'm no good to him dead. Would never be able to repay my debts then.' Ahmad laughed briefly, a sad, lonely laugh. 'I know what he meant. He meant Jafra, our daughter. He's got his eyes on her. Not to kill her, no. But to take her and hide her wherever he hides those other children, give her drugs, make her addicted. And then use her to earn money for him. We can't watch over her every minute of every day. Youssef would have found a way. He always finds a way. He knows the camp better than anyone else. I had to figure out how to pay my debts with Youssef quickly. And I had to find a way to protect our daughter, for ever. I had to find a powerful man, as powerful as Youssef, someone Youssef would not dare to cross. That's when I remembered that Abu Mahmoud had told me not long ago that he was looking for a new bride who could read the paper to him and massage his tired feet in the evenings. So I went to him. And we made a deal.'

Latifa now turns over, burying her nose in her daughter's long hair. How she wishes that Jafra was still a tiny tot whom she could protect with her own hands, her own power. But she can't. She can't. At least Abu Mahmoud was not violent towards his wives and children; at least that's what they say about him. And with a bit of luck, he will die soon. And then Jafra will be back with her. And Latifa will never let go of her daughter again.

Silent tears are streaming across Latifa's cheeks, and there is no way she can stop them.

Shatha

I lie on my bed watching television after yet another draining morning. But there really is no rest for the wicked; new orders are already reaching my ears. The only thing that ever changes around here is the chores I'm forced to do and the fun I'm ordered not to have.

'Shatha! Come and hang up the washing. And don't you dare drop anything.'

I turn the volume down and curse my luck for the umpteenth time. Her voice echoes through our apartment as I clamber out of bed. Welcome to Auntie Faten, my short, fat and frizzy-haired stepmother, with a heart as hard as her face.

The days roll into each other in our tiny home, where the rooms are locked in a tight embrace and the weary walls support one another. Damp seeps into them in the bitter winters. And whenever it rains, the water leaks through the ceilings, leaving patches of discoloured and peeling plaster. Here in the Shatila camp, we are the ones who have to support our walls and not the other way around.

*

I carefully drape the washing on the line on our small balcony, which overlooks a long and narrow street. It's the same street I used to play in as a little girl. I would lie flat on my belly on the ground, my small fists bulging with stones. My eyes would be open wide and then, as soon as the time was right, I would count to three and hurl my stash at seven stacked-up stones so I could knock over as many as possible and announce my victory. I would leap about dancing, whirling myself dizzy.

But now this young woman no longer wants to even look at the street. I'm bored senseless by the memories that pester me whenever I hang the washing out.

What I see now is a little boy stepping around objects that might hurt his brave bare feet. Already he seems like a wise old soul, having been forced to grow up too quickly. I hear an old man begging as he leans on a cane. He lost his right leg in the war. In a timid, trembling voice, he asks for help.

I finish Auntie Faten's latest chore and, as usual, I'm not thanked for my time or effort. And then I wait once again for details of my next assignment.

One of the worst things that can happen to a person is to be forced to live without goals. And the sign of ultimate failure is for them to live two identical days. As for me, my life is the epitome of failure.

I walk back to the kitchen to prepare some food for my old and ailing father. He has witnessed many battles, but the last one sidled up to him in the middle of the night, vowing not to let him leave without planting a kiss on his cheek first. Like a permanent tattoo, war dwells in his features.

Every pang he feels takes up residence in my heart. I sigh and I whisper a thousand prayers for his recovery. Oh, how my father's pain reverberates within me!

As for the harshness of war, I leave all of that within my stepmother's heart.

I tell Auntie Faten that I have decided to look for a job.

'But you've been looking for a job for months now,' she sneers. 'Ever since you graduated with your media degree. And they turn you down each time because of your nationality.'

We both sit silently after that, but inside I am raging. In this country, the subject of my 'nationality' has always made me feel like a pariah, or as though I'm being punished for something. But, no matter what, my pride remains intact. I have even applied for a scholarship to continue my studies at a Canadian university. But I would never utter a word about that to Auntie Faten. Now I repay her pessimistic glance with a bright smile.

'I'm not going to look for media jobs this time. I'm willing to do anything.'

Our reality is such that when we are young we are taught to be ambitious, study, go to university and follow our dreams professionally. Then, after we graduate, we discover that we will only be hired for a job that suits our nationality.

I drift to my bedroom, lost in a haze of despair. Something my mother used to always tell me when I was feeling particularly down about our camp wafts through my mind: 'Think of this dump as a work of art and you'll soon learn to appreciate it, for after destruction comes restoration. And after this refuge there will be a country for us again. After this camp, there will be a city named Haifa.'

I am still in awe of this great woman whose words constantly echo in my ears. Recalling them, I wander along the camp's alleyways, feeling secure as I create infinite paintings of the future in my mind.

Even during my lowest moments, I remember her smile, which faded and now lies beneath the dust. Remembering her bright face fills me with hope.

Her body embraces the earth and her soul the sky. And between the earth and the sky is a daughter trying desperately to follow in her footsteps.

Early next morning I head out job-hunting. Or at least that's what I tell my stepmother. But first I want to play my *nay*. With music in my heart I will more easily find the courage to once again knock on doors clutching my CV. But since I'm not allowed to play the *nay* at home – Auntie Faten hates me practising, she calls it 'noise' – I practise in the cultural centre at the other end of the camp.

Walking along our alleyway, which is narrow yet wide enough to hold a thousand stories, I wander down a lane that two people shouldn't be able to pass each other on. But ahead of me are two mothers, each gripping her child's hand. The women are strangers who have come across each other in the street. They invent an ingenious method of sliding past. Meanwhile, their children have become instant friends and are now holding hands, which makes their mothers smile.

The lane branches off into several broader streets at the top.

In the camp, I am bombarded by Auntie Faten's orders and the multitude of voices around me. I am only truly myself if I manage to find an empty room in the cultural centre to practise, so that with the help of the *nay* I can dissolve into the music and shut everything else out, or if I leave the camp altogether to sit in a park. That's when my thoughts truly belong to me.

At the centre I scan the noticeboard and come across a job advertisement for a position in a drug rehabilitation place just outside Shatila. It treats only Palestinians. I wonder if it has recently opened. My mother never mentioned it, even though she tried everything to help her brother, my uncle Ahmad.

I've always been aware of the dangers of drugs because of my uncle and my mother's attempts to help him when he was still a young man. But in recent years the drug problem in Shatila has become much more serious. While ten years ago my uncle was still an exception, nowadays young people take illegal drugs brazenly on the streets. Driven by a sense of despair and hopelessness, they see no other way out.

At the rehab centre, I find a job as a cook and cleaner, with a modest salary that will cover my father's treatment and anything else we need.

On my way back, I pass my mother's grave. Our souls embrace and I say a prayer for hers before walking home. The next day will be a very different one for me, and I need to get ready.

At the beginning, I find the work difficult. Everything is new and I feel anxious. For the first time in my life, I have to deal with strangers on a daily basis. There are so many people I don't know, from all walks of life: men, women, tall, short. There are the chirpy ones and the moody ones; people who thank me for the work I'm doing for them and people who simply ignore me. The fact that I am a woman and a young one at that, working in a place like this, serving them food, might be more than some of them can handle.

But what they don't know is how frightened I am of making a mistake and how paranoid I always feel. This insecurity is no doubt all down to Auntie Faten, who flares up at me at the slightest slip. And if I ever dare to raise my voice, her hand is there ready to slap me.

Yet I'm a good learner, getting the hang of things quickly. And before long I'm doing well. However difficult and tiring the work is, it is satisfying to know I am being paid for it. And the people are so friendly, it is a respite from my stepmother's constant orders.

There are fifteen people staying at the centre, nearly all of them young men. The only two girls are sisters, and this doesn't surprise me. In our culture, 'a boy can do no wrong', as they say. The fact that they are in a drug rehabilitation centre is nothing for them to be ashamed of. In fact, their family would proudly publicize how their son is receiving treatment. Yet if a girl says the wrong thing in passing, it could tarnish her reputation for ever. The families of the two female patients, Leila and Sahar, never visit them. They disowned them once they found out about their drug habit and their disgrace became public.

But all of them – boys and girls, men and women – bear the same wounds. Born bearing the burden of the Palestinian cause into a country which refuses to accept them as citizens, keeping them as refugees, as outcasts, they have grown up suffering. And once they complete their education with no hope of legal work, they find themselves on a dark and mysterious path where addiction is their only refuge. This is what our society offers us as an alternative reality. Uncle Ahmad fell into this trap as well, with no means of escape.

How lucky I am that I have my music, which allows me to transcend this grim reality and leave it all behind.

*

My job has given me confidence, and so I say yes when Mr Ghasif from the cultural centre proposes that I train with a singer for the talent show.

From the first time I play with Adam, I feel that the music we are creating is far larger, far more powerful than simply the *nay* and a human voice put together. We seem to create a magic bubble around us. And then this bubble becomes independent of us and carries us to a beautiful, weightless space. I've always played on my own, too shy to join others. Now I understand that playing on one's own is nothing more than practice. Only when you play with others are you making music.

After the talent show, something changed between Adam and me.

I can't stop thinking about him, even when we are not playing together. Or maybe especially when we are not playing together. When I'm at work, doing chores for Auntie Faten, walking through the camp. I don't notice the filthy streets any more, or all the sounds out there.

We meet up as often as we can, playing together, practising for our recording. Afterwards we sit on the roof at the cultural centre, drinking coffee. We both love Fairuz, the Lebanese singer, and we listen to her songs together while the sun is setting. We also discuss books. Adam is passionate about reading too.

Things become heated whenever we talk about our love for our country, Palestine, and we often play revolutionary songs together, by artists like Julia Boutros.

Adam talks to me about Syria and I tell him about the endurance of the people in Shatila and how kind-hearted they are.

As we sit on the roof at the centre, overlooking the camp, I notice how poorly maintained the place is. Most of the buildings haven't been touched since they were first built and their facades are deteriorating. But at least there is the vast sky above.

The buildings stand in rows like army convoys. Every day, they grow taller and taller, the only solution to house all the newcomers. The extensions make the buildings look like hands upraised as they beseech Allah to spare their lives, as someone drowning in a vast ocean might implore a saviour.

I can't read the expression on Adam's face as he stares at the camp. It seems to contain a mixture of aching and affection. As he takes a deep breath, I let out a long sigh, as if we are instinctively tending each other's wounds.

I tell him how I feel deeply conflicted when it comes to the camp. That I both love and despise it, that it bores me yet I long for it, how I reject it and desire it. In spite of its crumbling homes, streets and pavements, it oozes a substance that is capable of alleviating pain. It warms my heart when I see one of our number so innocently picking up a dropped morsel of food from the ground. How they give this wasted blessing a small kiss as they place it by the edge of the street so that no one steps on it, begging Allah for forgiveness. Or the smile of a child coming home from school. And the flags that decorate every inch of the camp and flutter in the breeze. No matter how many disagreements there are between the various residents of the camp, we are all united in our love for Palestine.

I glance at the camp once again, as if I'm seeing it for the first time. I still discover something new about it each time I look. And it seems different depending on where you look at it from. The camp is a treasure trove of secrets.

For the first time ever, nothing troubles me as I walk down the usual streets. With Adam in my life, our pavements gleam. The children are all grinning. The old beggar is fit and healthy. Adam's smile miraculously wipes the sweat off the brow of a weary labourer. Through him, I learn that the problem isn't in what we see but how we see it.

With each passing day, I become increasingly attached to Adam. I scold myself. How can that be! He's three years younger than me. Yet he appears so mature. The overwhelming affection I feel for him makes it seem like he is a piece of ribbon holding my soul together. Were the ribbon to tear, my soul would be scattered. Whenever Adam laughs, his laughter smashes through the chains around my heart. And whenever Adam sings, I breathe in the dusty air of Palestine and lose myself in the embrace of my homeland.

This is the first time I have ever been gripped by such feelings. Since love is something to be ashamed of here, I am terrified that Auntie Faten will find out and force me to stop working, or going out at all. If anyone ever finds out that a girl here is in love, their disparaging words would eventually destroy any spirit she had left. And she would simply become a hollow shell, an object for every wagging tongue.

Every morning, after getting ready to leave for work, my heart races me down the long staircase. The whole camp smiles back at me. Love transforms depressing cities into streets of blossoming flowers.

In the afternoon, when I reach the centre, I stop for a while and watch Adam from afar, mesmerized by the way he caresses the pages of a book as if they were his lover. And how his face changes from joy to sorrow as he reads, making me wonder what secrets lie between those lines.

Although Adam tells me he doesn't use social media apart from on rare occasions, he sends me messages all night long, which makes me even more confused about his feelings towards me.

Winter winds its way into our days and we bid farewell to the scorching summer. The rain also interferes with our online chats as the internet signal becomes shaky with the bad weather. On those nights, Adam and I exchange a single message just to check the other is well. But as soon as the signal improves, we chat for hours on end.

To him, my hair is like 'strands of gold fallen from Palestine's sun'. 'It complements,' he muses, 'your blue eyes, which are like the blue sea of Jaffa, which never sleeps.'

I hang on his every word, then mull over them for hours, trying to deduce their real meaning.

As for me, there is no way I will tell him that I love him. I was born into a society where a girl must speak in hushed tones, never laugh out loud and always walk with her gaze lowered in public.

So instead I say, 'In the middle of a very tiring day, I thought of you and smiled.' Or I might tell him how he helped me to find the strength to cope with my father's pain. And how, thanks to him, Auntie Faten's orders now flutter about my ears like falling petals.

Meeting Adam is one of the best things to have ever happened to me. Because of him, my life has become full of ambition again. He has brightened my days and his love has given me a renewed passion for life. Which means that when I receive the offer from the Canadian university, including a visa to travel, at first I'm so shocked, so confused, that I can't even remember having applied. But I did apply. Before Adam's arrival. Never expecting to receive such a chance.

The Wedding Day

Jafra has no clue what is going to happen to her today. She's thrilled because her mother has encouraged her to invite Mais over, and now she's even helping them to apply make-up. Jafra's mother is so much better at it than the girls. It's probably what you learn when you're grown up, Jafra thinks to herself.

'Look, how pretty. Like two proper young ladies.'

Latifa is holding up the big mirror so that the girls can admire their beaming reflections. Jafra is wearing her new white dress, and Mais a blue one her mother bought her instead of the white.

'I don't want her to know,' Latifa said to Ahmad. 'What good will it do if we destroy the last few days of her childhood? She has no choice. I have no choice.'

She didn't say, Ahmad has no choice. He had a choice. Oh yes! Years ago, when he chose drinking and drugs.

Now Latifa pretends she has to sneeze, turning her head away from the girls. She doesn't want them to notice how her eyes have filled with tears.

She's deceitful, she's betraying her own daughter. But what can she do? Ahmad is right, they have to protect the girl from Youssef. Heartless Youssef, the unelected leader of the camp.

Ahmad calls his wife into the kitchen.

'The sheikh will be here in half an hour,' he whispers.

He's organized for the local imam to come to their house first to receive the vows of the bride, then the holy man will head to Abu Mahmoud to finalize the marriage.

'And stuff Jafra's dress with some padding around the chest, will you?' Ahmad continues. 'Her body needs to appear more mature. I'm worried that the sheikh might refuse to go ahead otherwise.'

Without a glance at her husband, Latifa heads back to the girls. She will obey her husband's command, prepare Jafra, but she will make sure he senses her contempt.

'You look just like an *arousa*, a bride, my darling.' Latifa raises her right hand to the top of her mouth and breaks into a joyous ululation.

The two girls double over laughing.

'How about pretending it's a real wedding?' Latifa then exclaims, as if that thought has just crossed her mind.

'Oh, yes! But how shall we do that, Mama? There's no groom.' Again both girls break into fits of giggles.

'And no sheikh,' Mais then adds, catching her breath. She of course knows all about weddings, since she's just been to her uncle's.

'I put up a screen here.' Latifa points to a spot near the door. 'Your father has a friend coming shortly, and he will pretend to be the sheikh.'

Oh, how evil Latifa feels. But it will all be over in the next hour and then she can begin to hope that Abu Mahmoud will die soon. And she will visit her daughter every day.

Jafra is sitting on a wooden chair behind the screen. She's hiding her naked feet underneath her long dress. The naked feet are the only part that don't belong to a real bride. But her mother suddenly rushed her: 'Your father's friend is here. Quick, sit down.' And so Jafra had no time to find her good pair of shoes. But it doesn't matter really, because in every other sense she feels like a proper bride. She hears a commotion behind the screen, followed by a sonorous voice.

'Do you agree to this marriage with conviction and without coercion?'

'Yes,' she replies, trying to make her voice sound deeper, like that of a woman. 'Yes, I agree.'

Mais is standing beside her, pressing her hands against her mouth to stifle the giggles. 'They asked my uncle's bride exactly the same question,' she squeaks.

Latifa fetches something to eat for the girls and then suggests they go for a walk.

'Like this?' Jafra asks, surprised, pointing to her face and Mais's, painted like grown-up women. Shyness has suddenly overcome her. Won't the other children laugh at them?

'They won't even recognize you, my darling,' Latifa assures her daughter. 'And your father will come too. He'll sort them out if anyone dares to poke fun.'

When they reach Abu Mahmoud's house they stop. Without knocking, Jafra's dad opens the front door. Jafra hesitates. Why are they here?

'Come inside,' Ahmad says, looking at his daughter. 'Mais, you wait here.'

Jafra doesn't at all like the tone of her father's voice. She recognizes the same hint of menace that comes when he's about to beat her. But her thoughts are interrupted by her mother, who takes Jafra's face between her trembling hands and then pulls the girl close. Jafra notices tears in her mother's eyes.

'Forgive me, my daughter,' whispers Latifa.

Canada Calling

Before my father became too ill to walk about every day, he and I would visit my mother's grave most Friday mornings at five o'clock. It was our time together. Sometimes we talked and sometimes we simply enjoyed our shared longing for my mother in silence.

'Do you have any plans after finishing your degree this summer?' my father asked, handing me his cane and taking the full pitcher from my other hand.

I kept silent, pretending to watch him sprinkling water over the grave.

'Would you like to continue with a master's?' he added.

I shook my head, avoiding my father's eyes. I knew he would find the money if I were to say yes. Even if Auntie Faten raged about the waste of it all. She, and of course we too, knew that even a master's wouldn't get me a job. There are no jobs for Palestinians in Lebanon.

My father read Surah Yaseen, then prayed. I sat down on the ground and watched him. I had thought about my future, but I didn't know how to broach the subject with him. I knew in advance it would not be an easy conversation. He prostrated himself once more, then sat up straight on his knees. I took a deep breath. Being close to my mother here by her grave gave me courage. She would understand my wish and support me in following my dreams.

'A Canadian university's offering scholarships for Arab students to earn their master's degree in different fields, including media studies. I'd like to apply.'

'Why?' With a sudden impatient flick of his head, my father hinted that I should help him up. I went to stand behind him and lifted him onto his feet.

'You know that I won't get a job here with my Palestinian ID,' I said quietly. 'And so I thought...' I stopped, hesitating. My father already looked angry. What I was about to say would put him in an even worse mood. But I had to say it now. 'And so I thought that maybe if I could do a postgraduate degree in Canada, I might be able to work there for a few years afterwards.' I handed my father his cane.

'You don't speak English well enough.' He began to walk away, his cane hitting the ground hard.

For a moment I walked beside him without saying anything. Then: 'English proficiency classes are part of the programme.'

Tok – tok – tok. The noise of his cane was all I heard for a while.

'Only cowards leave,' he suddenly hissed through tight lips. 'Only cowards long for a life of luxury and abandon the Palestinian cause.'

I felt close to tears.

'Our family's always been part of the resistance.' He pushed the words out of his angry mouth. 'Your family defended and protected our people in this camp for decades. And now you want to just leave and abandon everything! That's not how I raised you.'

'I will come back.'

More than ever I wanted my mother to be here. She would have understood and found the right words to explain everything to my father.

'I also want to help our people. But to do that I need to get experience and expertise. Then I… we can achieve much more.'

My father didn't reply. And he didn't speak to me for the rest of our walk home.

After that he never raised the subject again.

And nor did I.

But I submitted my application. And then forgot about it. And now I have met Adam. And my father is not at all well.

For the next few days I pretend that the email with the scholarship offer is not sitting in my inbox. I'm hoping that I might forget it until it's too late to reply. Or maybe it's spam? This thought rushes into my mind as I leave work to meet Adam in the cultural centre to practise for our recording. I message him, say my father needs me at home. I will meet him tomorrow instead. Suddenly the idea that maybe there is no real offer from the Canadian university is more unbearable than having been presented with such an opportunity, such a difficult decision to make. I rush home. Of course I could have checked my inbox on my phone out on the street. But I want to be on my own.

The email is not spam, and I still have time to accept.

'I've been offered a scholarship by Canada to continue my studies there,' I say.

Adam and I are sitting on the roof of the cultural centre, drinking coffee. Our shoulders are touching while we stare out at the setting sun. A moment ago I still felt his shoulders gently lifting up and down to the rhythm of his breathing. Now they have stopped moving.

While we practised downstairs I couldn't concentrate. I felt under such pressure, my heart racing ever since I made the decision last night that I wanted to talk to Adam about it.

My eyes latch on to a large iron key fixed to the UNRWA water tower opposite the building we are sitting on top of. This key symbolizes all the keys that our Palestinian families took with them in 1948 when they had to leave our homeland, believing that they would soon be able to return and once again unlock their front doors. Every family I know still has their old house key.

I'm waiting for Adam to say something. I don't know why I'm so scared. Yes, I do know why. I'm scared of his reaction.

'I will miss you,' he says eventually. 'But maybe we can stay in touch?' he then adds, almost inaudibly.

'So you think I should go?' I ask.

Was that what I had hoped for, for him to encourage me to go? Or had I wanted him to tell me to stay? I don't know. There is a numbness inside me and so much confusion.

'You have to go.' His voice is husky, the words come out trembling. He clears his throat. 'You have to go,' he repeats, more firmly, more in control of himself.

All of a sudden a huge wave of relief washes over me. As a friend he says I have to go, as a lover he says he doesn't want to lose me.

My hands have been clasping the coffee cup in my lap so tightly that my fingernails have burrowed into my palms. I now release my grip. I want to feel more of Adam than just his shoulder skimming against mine. But I hesitate. What if someone sees us?

His fingertips carefully touch the back of my right hand.

I turn my palm upwards and our fingers interlink.

We don't speak.

Maybe a minute, maybe five. A beautiful eternity that will never end.

'Maybe we can stay in touch?' Adam asks again.

'Maybe you can apply too and follow me? You're going to finish school in the summer,' I say. Everything seems possible.

My father is sitting on his bed. He grabs hold of his cane with his right hand and places his left hand over the right. Then he slowly lowers his head to rest on his hands. I am kneeling in front of him, crying. I'm hurting my father and I never wanted to hurt him. I have told him that I've accepted the Canadian university offer.

'Our nation's cause is only one reason why I don't want you to leave,' my father now says. 'I don't want to die with you far away. I want you to be near me. I want to see my grandchildren coming into this world.'

When I was a little girl I used to lie in bed with my eyes wide open after my mother had said goodnight to me. I would be waiting for my father, and by forcing my eyes to remain open without blinking I wanted to stop myself from falling asleep. As soon as I heard the door, I'd jump up and run to my dad. He would then sit down with me on our soft carpet, pulling me onto his lap, and I'd disappear inside his deep, warm embrace. There I felt a sense of deep belonging. I would settle my small body on his crossed legs and rest my head on his left shoulder, eavesdropping on his heartbeats. As for my hands, one of them would be stroking his neck. The other rested in his palms as he massaged my fingers, one by one, passing them over his full, soft lips. He would plant a little kiss on each stubby finger and then carry on massaging them while telling me the story of the man who dared his children to snap a stick in half. Once they had managed to break it, the man then dared them to break the whole bundle of sticks, but they couldn't. The story ends with a phrase about how a stick is protected by its bundle and how weak it is alone. And just before tucking me back into bed, he'd sing 'Tik, Tik, Ya Em Slaiman' and 'Fly, Kite, Fly' by Fairuz.

Now I lift myself up from the floor and sit down next to my father on the bed. I would love to put my arm around him but I don't dare.

'Baba, please. I have to go.'

Inside, my heart is breaking.

The next day I receive a WhatsApp message from Adam in the middle of the afternoon, asking me if I can meet him urgently as soon as I've finished at work. My heart starts racing. I freshen up quickly and hurry to meet him, speeding through the streets without stopping to look at anything.

Adam is at our agreed meeting point with a backpack at his feet. He turns when I call out his name.

'I won't keep you long,' he says, out of breath, as if he'd been running. He kneels down to open his bag. He takes out a book and hands it to me. *Love in the Time of War.*

'I've read it five times or maybe more,' he says, blushing. 'I want you to have it.' Then he says, 'I love you.'

And before I can say anything, he turns and disappears down the street.

No Man

The next morning, I walk to school with my head in the clouds and my feet oblivious to the puddles they are walking through. It rained heavily last night. But I'm not bothered by that. I'm driven by a new determination to finish my last school year's exams well. I have four more months, and during that time I will study hard so that I can apply for the Canadian scholarship and follow Shatha. I spent until the early hours of the morning reading up about it online.

As I pass Youssef's café, a sudden clamour to my right pulls me out of my daydream. It's the alley where Shatha lives. I stop to see what's happened. There is shouting.

'*Ya Allah!*'

'Come on, people. Someone send for a car or motorbike quickly! Get away from her! Move, move!'

A crowd of men, women, young and old, are huddled around someone on the ground. I pick up some of what they're saying over the din.

'Allah is sufficient for us and He is the best of protectors! May Allah give us the patience to carry on. May He punish the people behind this calamity.'

'Come on. We need to help her! Where's that motorbike?'

Suddenly, as if pushed by an invisible hand and with a gut-wrenching sense of foreboding inside me, I press through the crowd, shoving people out of my way until I see her.

Shatha is sprawled on the ground, unconscious. I stand frozen to the spot, not blinking as my brain races to try and make sense of what my startled eyes are seeing.

'Shatha!' I hear myself screaming, tearing me out of my state. I collapse next to her, grab her head and start to shake it.

'Shatha, say something!' I scream, all the while shaking her listless body.

'Shatha, don't leave me. Open your eyes. Shatha, please!'

The desperate voice of an old man reaches me.

'Where's Shatha? Where is my girl?'

The crowd parts to let a man hunched deep over a cane through. I recognize him as Shatha's father, whom I had met at the talent show. Someone pulls me away from Shatha. Then Youssef, the drug lord of the camp, appears next to Shatha's dad. I process everything as if watching scenes from a movie. This isn't real. This can't be real. Shatha on the ground, she's not moving. Youssef talks to Shatha's father. Then he bends down, picks up her body and carries her quickly to the end of the lane where his car is parked. I follow them and without thinking or hesitating squeeze into the back seat with Shatha and her father. Youssef is already behind the steering wheel. The car begins to move. I slam the door shut next to me. For a fleeting moment, Shatha's father's and my eyes meet. No army will be able to remove me from this car. Shatha's father indicates his consent with a brief nod.

Shatha's feet are resting in my lap, while her head is raised on her father's as he cradles her face between his palms.

'Get up, daughter!' he shouts. 'Wake up, please, I'm begging you. Allah, please don't take my daughter away from me!'

Throngs of people from the camp are chasing after our car. But luckily, in front of us the crowds are parting as they see Youssef's car, which everyone knows, racing towards the camp's exit.

Outside, heavy traffic slows us down and Youssef quickly loses his temper.

'Clear the way, people!' he shouts out of the window at the other drivers. 'This is an emergency! Get out of the way!'

When we finally reach the Makassed General Hospital in the nearby Tariq al Jadidah district, the car screeches to a halt and we stumble out, carrying Shatha down the hospital corridors. The doctors stop us from following them into the critical care unit as they take her through.

I look around at the countless questioning gazes directed at me from all the other people who have gathered in the corridor. Questions are hurled into the air.

'What happened to her?'

'Has the doctor seen her?'

'How did this happen?'

'She was electrocuted when she touched a wall.'

'Be patient, Abu Shatha. Your daughter will be OK, *inshallah*.'

The din rattles my brain and I sit with my back against the wall, shaking with fear over the fate of Shatha, my first and only true friend in the camp. My first and only love.

Cutting through the commotion is the reverberation of my heart, which pounds as though a bomb has just ripped it apart.

We are forced to sit and wait for the doctor's diagnosis. Never in my life have I detested waiting as much as I do right now.

I look around at the worried faces surrounding me, stare into their confused eyes and listen to the sound of Abu Shatha's agonizing sighs. A shiver runs through my entire body as the sound of Auntie Faten's piercing screams reach us from the other end of the corridor.

'Shatha! *Habibti!* Where is she? Tell me, where is she?' she wails, tears gushing from her eyes.

Her husband gathers her in his arms to try and console her. The others join in with soothing words or phrases as they collectively say prayers for the safety of their daughter.

*

A dizziness takes hold of me, forcing my eyes shut as everything around me turns to blackness. Dark memories I will never be able to forget are awakened from the recesses of my brain. Images flash through my mind too fast for me to stop. I see Yarmouk Street in the Yarmouk refugee camp where I was born.

I see thousands of the camp's residents swarming towards the entrance on that dreadful morning of 17 December 2012. Their faces are visions of bitterness and heartbreak at being forced out of their homes.

It is as though the whole street is weeping, as it marches alongside its families and children. The scene is an embodiment of hope's ultimate defeat after evil has conquered justice.

Yarmouk, the largest Palestinian camp in Syria, which had been a refuge for the multitudes fleeing the ill-fated neighbouring regions, was itself no longer safe. The previous day, just half an hour after the Free Syrian Army entered the camp, it was bombed by the regime's MiG aircraft.

Women, men, children, the young, the old, babes in arms… everyone flees the camp, walking shadows of their former selves. Along with their belongings, they are also leaving behind their souls. These I can see hanging on the walls and from the windows of their abandoned homes.

The scene reminds me of the stories my grandfather told me about how they were forced to flee Palestine over half a century ago. To one side of me, I see a man walking along with his frail, elderly mother on his back, weighed down by the added burden of their bags. On the other, a man carries his two crying daughters in his arms, a large bag on his back.

'*Ya Allah*, where will we go when we don't know anyone out there?' this man mourns.

An elderly woman staggers along, balancing a large bundle on her head. It includes the clothes of her only son, who had been martyred. Wrapped in there too are her dreams of one day returning to her country, which her son had sacrificed himself for. 'This is our second exodus,' she mutters, bitter tears falling from her bloodshot eyes. 'This is our second Nakba. Our camp, our country... Where are you, our country, to draw us into your bosom?'

An elderly man standing on the other side of the street, surveying the scene and the columns of people marching all in the same direction, starts crying out, '*Ya Allah!* This is the Day of Reckoning, the Day of Reckoning! Why is this happening to us? Why, *ya Allah*, why? Where are we going? *Ya Allah*. Where is there for us to go? I swear, we are so tired.'

A woman weeps as she tries to drag her son by the hand so they can leave the camp, but he's putting up a strong fight. 'Mama,' he pleads. 'Let's stay. These are our homes. This is our camp. Come on! Where are we going to go? Wherever we go we'll be humiliated and treated even worse than we are now. Let's just stay here and let the bombs fall. Trust me, it'll be a kinder death.'

As for me, I am in a car. With my sister, Reham, her husband, Marwan, and my parents. I watch the events unfolding in front of my eyes and I suddenly realize that the place that has so far encapsulated my youth and which was my first experience of belonging is no longer mine.

It feels as though someone is gouging out a part of me and tearing me away from my own self. My tears erupt, but I don't feel the stinging until I glance over at my mother and see her green eyes weeping in excruciating silence. I bury my face in her shoulder.

'Shatha is dead.'

My body shudders and I look up, startled.

'Shatha is dead,' the doctor repeats. 'May Allah rest her soul.'

And then I'm up on my feet, digging my fingers in his arm and screaming at him. 'No! Doctor, please! For God's sake, do something. Shatha can't die.'

One of the other men grabs me and pulls me towards him to try and calm me down as I continue to scream hysterically.

'Get your hands off me! Shatha wants to live! Shatha! Come out of that room! Shatha!'

Shatha's stepmother faints as soon as she hears Shatha's name uttered in the same breath as the word 'death'. Her father, looking bereft, his spirit broken, stands motionless.

When I walk into our apartment my mother, who has already heard the news from other people in the camp, rushes towards me and hugs me tightly. We don't say a word, so as not to disrupt the solemnity of the silence surrounding us.

Leading me by the hand to my bedroom, she helps me find some black clothes to wear. I am unaware of what is happening around me, my whole body as immobile as a statue sculpted to face in only one direction. Then she leads me to the front door.

'Be a man,' she says, as she opens the door and gives me a gentle nudge.

I make my way down the narrow, dingy stairs, one of many identical stairways in the camp, with its exposed concrete steps. At a pace as slow and steady as the ticking of a clock, my feet land heavily on each step, shaking my eerily immobile features to life. Tears trickle through the eyelashes of my unblinking eyes, which feel as cold as my arteries when I donate blood.

The tears dry on my cheeks as I reach the door of our building.

I see a huge crowd gathered in the alleyway outside Shatha's building. The faces of everyone seem overcast: children, teenagers, middle-aged and elderly men, women. I imagine that I can see my reflection in their faces, each carrying a little of the bitterness I feel.

Eight men appear, led by Shatha's father and uncle, carrying the coffin and struggling to squeeze it through the narrow entrance.

As they pass right in front of me, the others begin to follow them. I join them for two steps before stopping and letting them overtake me. Overhead, I see the electrical cables hanging above us, then I step forward and we walk together.

We leave the alley behind us and reach one of the main streets. Someone in the group begins chanting, 'There is no God but Allah! And Allah loves martyrs,' which everyone else repeats.

I walk with measured steps along with the crowds and their chanting. Among them are some of the camp's security officials and the heads of charities and organizations. I spot some of the officials who are supposed to be in charge of the electricity problem in the camp, but who instead pocket the money sent by foreign investors and Europeans to solve the electricity crisis. I see Muneef. He acknowledges me with a nod.

But Shatha isn't there. She is nowhere to be seen.

I remember my mother's words, 'Be a man.'

As the people walk on, I stay where I am. Then I turn back and walk home.

I am no man without my friend by my side.

An Angel by My Side

At the beginning I thought we all – my parents, Adam, Marwan and I – would only be in Shatila, or indeed in Lebanon, for a short while. How naive I was.

I hated the camp. From the very first week, it was obvious that I rejected life in Shatila. Despite how small it is, it still took me a long time to get around. I used its walls as markings in the hope that they would guide me. I memorized the drawings on the walls of the children's nursery or charity and social organizations and the UNRWA school. I lived here in the hope of leaving.

Slowly, my personality began to change and my voice became louder. I started to put on weight. And after a few months I had turned into an expert in stealing the salty water from the neighbours' storage containers and in tracing the electrical cable that had been stolen from our home.

And then something happened. I signed up for a computer course. They were offered for free to refugees in the camp. The teacher, Mr Amr, was a kind man who reminded me of my uncle Abu Hamza. My mood began to improve. Glory be to Allah who enables us to forget our trials.

'I want to work.'

'What!' Marwan shouts as he puts down his fork. He loses his temper totally, screaming that he's probably the only man in the camp who has work outside and now I, his wife, dares ask him to let me work, and who said we needed money and what kind of a job did I expect to get when I only just scraped through my tenth grade? And anyway I'm nothing but a Palestinian refugee here in Lebanon.

I expected this reaction from my husband and I am not at all surprised. Still, I pretend to be hurt and storm off to the bedroom and slam the door shut.

For the following two days neither of us speaks a word to the other. Yet from the beginning I've bet that by the third day Marwan will come and apologize and tell me to go ahead and get the best job at a company that will be lucky to have me. And that even though jobs here are like gold dust, he will still ask around his friends and see if they can help him. I have also decided that I will tell him about other courses that are available and will suggest I call Mr Amr, my teacher, to see if he can help me. I've always suspected that this will make my husband so jealous that he will say something along the lines of how he, Marwan, manages multiple projects and is more than capable of helping his wife to get a job.

And so, as predicted, on the third day Marwan starts to soften and tries to placate me, but I stick to my guns. A whole week passes this way and then, just as he's done previously when he placed the bus ticket to my parents' home on the bed, this time he lays a printout of a job description beside me. He used my documents to fill in an application form for me. The job he's found is as a cook and cleaner in a drug rehabilitation centre. For a second my heart stops as I realize it's the job Adam's friend Shatha did until her death. Marwan never knew about Shatha and Adam.

My husband is of course unhappy about the environment I will be entering with this job and he also doesn't like the work I'll be doing, but it's the only thing he could find, and after all he wants to see me content so we can continue pretending we are just like a normal couple.

I enjoy every minute of my job. I love being with different people and experiencing the satisfaction of completing a task well. Every assignment, every opportunity that is handed to me, I take. And I save the money I earn. And the more I save, the clearer an image becomes in my head: I can stand on my own two feet. I don't need Marwan. If my parents won't take me back I will find a place of my own. Truth be told, I don't think it through completely. But that's beside the point. I am now determined to leave Marwan.

*

That evening I talk to my husband. I tell him that to this day I haven't forgiven him for what he did to me after I gave birth. He denied me the happiness any woman wishes to experience. And he cold-heartedly made a victim of my daughter. My life ended the day Malaak, my little angel, died, may Allah rest her soul. My feelings for him died that day too. And my own heart died. Dead. Gone.

'I don't understand,' he says. 'I thought we'd put all that behind us a long time ago.'

'I want a divorce,' I say calmly.

Marwan punches the wall with his fist, accusing me of losing my mind, that I don't know what I'm talking about, that he will forbid me to work.

He hurls himself at me like a madman and starts to beat me. I cry and scream, but can't fight him off. He continues to beat me, threatening to slit my throat. I cower in a corner, trying to protect my head with my raised arms. Suddenly the neighbours bang on the door. I hoped they would. In Shatila we all live so close together and the walls are so poorly constructed that there's no sense of privacy. Everyone knows everything about each other. And many people turn violent here – men against women, women against their children – as the only means of exerting control, and so neighbours are used to having to interfere to prevent the worst from happening. I race to the door, open it and collapse onto the ground behind them. They grab Marwan and pull him away from me, then tell me to go and cover myself.

I pull a dress over my nightgown and tie a scarf round my head. I've prepared a small bag with some clothes, my gold jewellery and important documents earlier. I take the bag and stay at our neighbours' apartment until it's light outside, so I can go to the sharia court.

Despite my mother's many attempts over the phone and WhatsApp and Skype all night long to convince me to go back to Marwan, I head to the sharia court the following day and speak to several lawyers, asking for their help in carrying out the divorce. They advise me to raise a petition of separation on the condition that I surrender all my rights to my husband. I agree without hesitation. In the next few days Marwan tries to call me over and over again, but my conscience doesn't allow me to answer. My daughter's image is carved in my memory and heart. When Marwan can't persuade me to hear him out, he sends me a message on WhatsApp: 'I have to see you about something important.' I reply that I will see him in court.

At the hearing, Marwan and I stand facing the sharia judge, who tries to persuade me to return to my husband. But after I insist that I won't go back to him, and that I am willing to give up all my rights, including returning my dowry, he turns to Marwan and asks him to deliver the divorce declaration. Marwan stutters, his eyes filling with tears, his lips trembling. He can't say a word and glances at me like a broken man, pleading with me to take pity on him. I begin to feel sorry for him and his underlying regret. The judge repeats the request to Marwan, who answers huskily that if this is her wish and she won't change her mind, then he agrees. But he asks me to keep the dowry, saying he won't let me return it. Addressing the judge, I accept these terms and request to donate my dowry to the drug rehabilitation centre.

I leave the court hugging the divorce certificate like a trophy.

And Malaak, my little angel, is smiling down on me.

Afterword

I arrived in the UK in 1998 as a 25-year-old woman. I came from an ambitious, middle-class Syrian family. We lived in Damascus and I was lucky enough to be allowed to travel abroad. I wanted to explore different ways of living, here in the West. I was attracted by the civilized conditions for women, their freedom of expression and the norms of social tolerance.

I found a job washing dishes in a London pub and eventually I went back to university to obtain a master's in international relations. Every year I used to travel to Syria for a few weeks to visit my family and friends. And when my children were born I took them with me to teach them about their Arabic roots.

In 2011, when the Syrian conflict broke out, I was far away from the apple and mulberry trees where I grew up. I was far away from Damascus and the heady intoxicating scent of jasmine. I was separated from my family, my nephews and my friends, from people whom I love, cherish and admire. And these people are still there inside the war zone, risking indiscriminate destruction. Every day I have felt guilty because I live in safety while they live in danger.

During the last seven years I have visited Syria twice. My family has moved from Damascus to a village. Some of my friends have fled the country to Lebanon and Europe; others have disappeared and I don't know whether they are alive or dead.

When Meike invited me to work on this book, I felt excited. I could finally do something by giving my compatriots the chance to tell their own story. Yet as we arrived in Shatila I became anxious. The possibility of meeting people I might know or recognize made my heart beat faster. I was frightened to see the pain in their eyes.

Some of the writers we worked with are Palestinian Syrians who come from the Yarmouk Palestinian camp in Damascus. The images of the devastated Yarmouk streets that appeared on the front pages of Western newspapers surged back to my mind. In the 1990s I used to visit Yarmouk almost every day because my best friends lived there. We were all part of a liberal movement. I would carry the Palestinian flag in support of their intifada. I remember the famous Al Nejmah (Star) bakery in Safad Street and can picture the square with the children's playground. I know the alleyways where fresh groceries were arranged daily on market stalls. I can still hear the Palestinian housewives haggling over prices.

A couple of other writers came from different areas of Syria. I hesitated to ask Nibal, who lived in Deir el-Zour, about my friend Alim. Alim and I used to argue for hours about travel abroad. He would tell me, 'Don't run away. If you want to make a change, make it in your own country.' We lost touch in 2012. When eventually I asked, Nibal sighed. She knew him well. Her voice broke: 'He's still in Damascus, drinking arak, writing dark poems, observing Damascus' narrow streets, hearing shells day and night and seeing blood everywhere.'

At times I could not look our refugee writers in the eye. I felt ashamed by the privilege of my position. I could have been them; they could have been me. I tried to ease my discomfort by telling them about my friends still living in Syria. But whatever I said, I still felt like an outsider – someone who came to work with them for a few weeks and then flew back to London.

Since that time, I have started to work with Syrian refugees here in the UK. I help them to integrate, to find housing and to negotiate the maze of bureaucracy. Working with refugees in Britain has presented new challenges for me. I am faced every day with people who feel isolated; people who have to deal with traumas caused by war and flight; people who are thrust into situations they need to understand without the appropriate language or the relevant experience.

And yet I have discovered that, for some refugees, the experience of being forced to leave their culture, their environment, their comfort zone, presents unforeseen opportunities. I have met women who feel liberated and finally able to follow their interests. For example, the mother of one writer is my age. She was married when she was twelve. She is now a widow, a refugee, with four children. But for the first time in her life she can do what she always wanted to do: take acting classes.

Thanks to our project in Shatila, I have met nine remarkable writers. Without the conflict, they would not, perhaps, have had stories to tell. Now that you have read their words, I trust that you will marvel at their honesty, their humanity and their surprising literary skill. I'm proud to be one of the people to help these writers find the audience they deserve.

SUHIR HELAL

editor, Shatila Stories

Authors

OMAR KHALED AHMAD is Palestinian Syrian. He was born in 1998 in the Yarmouk camp in Damascus. In 2013 he fled the Syrian crisis and moved with his family to Shatila, Beirut. In 2016 he studied video journalism with the German Academy of the Deutsche Welle and now works for Shatila's Campji, a youth media electronic platform for refugees. Omar has also directed a short film about life inside the Shatila camp.

NIBAL ALALO is Syrian. She was born in 1975 in Deir ez-Zour. She obtained a master's in sociology and worked for eleven years as a psychosocial support worker with Iraqi refugees in Damascus. She moved to Beirut in 2015 because of the war and is now working with Syrian refugees in the Shatila camp.

SAFA KHALED ALGHARBAWI is Syrian. She was born in 1990 in Damascus and has lived in the Shatila camp since 2013. She has a higher national diploma in economics.

OMAR ABDELLATIF ALNDAF is Syrian. He was born in 1989 in Idlib, where he also obtained a diploma in aluminium and glass production. He fled to Lebanon in 2011. He loves Arabic poetry.

RAYAN MOHAMAD SUKKAR is Palestinian Lebanese. She was born in 1995 in the Shatila camp. She currently studies media at the Arab University of Beirut. In 2016 she completed a one-year course in video journalism with the German Academy of the Deutsche Welle and now works for Shatila's Campji. She has also co-authored the play *Tarah Bedda* with the Ebaad organization and worked as an assistant director for a play at the American University in Beirut.

SAFIYA BADRAN is Syrian. She was born in 1986 and came to Beirut in 2011. She works for the NGO Basmeh & Zeitooneh in the Shatila camp.

FATIMA OMAR GHAZAWI is Palestinian Lebanese. She was born in 1997 in the Shatila camp. She is currently studying psychology at the Lebanese University and is a freelance writer for the magazine *Wammda*.

SAMIH MAHMOUD is Palestinian Syrian. He was born in 1998 in the Yarmouk camp in Damascus. He moved with his family to the Shatila camp in 2013. In 2016 he completed a one-year course in video journalism with the German Academy of the Deutsche Welle and now works for Shatila's Campji.

HIBA MAREB is Palestinian Syrian. She was born in 1987 in the Yarmouk camp in Damascus. For three years she studied psychology at the Faculty of Education in Damascus before the Syrian crisis forced her to move to Beirut in 2012. She now works as a tutor in adult education in the Shatila camp. Hiba also co-authored *The History of the Puppet Theatre in Lebanese Arabic Theatre*.

Translator

NASHWA GOWANLOCK is a British Egyptian writer, journalist and translator of Arabic literature. She is the co-translator with Ruth Ahmedzai Kemp of *The Crossing: My Journey to the Shattered Heart of Syria* by Samar Yazbek. Her translation of Abdelrashid Mahmoudi's novel *After Coffee* is published by HBKU Press.

Nashwa would like to thank Niam Itani for her invaluable help with the translation.

Thank you

Meike and Suhir would like to thank the 327 readers who responded to our Kickstarter funding call for this project. Without your incredibly generous support this book would not have been possible. Shukran.

We also would like to thank the photographer Paul Romans, who accompanied us on our second visit to Shatila.

BASMEH & ZEITOONEH
RELIEF & DEVELOPMENT

Peirene is proud to support Basmeh & Zeitooneh.

Basmeh & Zeitooneh (The Smile & The Olive) is a Lebanese-registered NGO. It was established in 2012 in response to the Syrian refugee crisis. B&Z aims to create opportunities for refugees to move beyond being victims of conflict and help them to become empowered individuals who one day will return to their own country to rebuild their society. Today the organization is managing nine community centres in the region: seven in Lebanon and two in Turkey.

Peirene will donate 50p from the sale of this book to the charity. Thank you for buying this book.

www.basmeh-zeitooneh.org